The Hardy Boys Mysteries

FREE GIFTS FROM
THE ARMADA COLLECTORS' CLUB

Look out for these tokens in your favourite Armada series! All you need to do to receive a special FREE GIFT is collect 6 tokens in the same series and send them off to the address below with a postcard marked with your name and address including postcode. Start collecting today!

Send your tokens to:

Armada Collectors' Club
HarperCollins Children's Books,
77 - 85 Fulham Palace Road,
London, W6 8JB

Or if you live in New Zealand to:

Armada Collectors' Club
HarperCollins Publishers Ltd.
31 View Road, Glenfield,
PO Box 1, Auckland

THIS OFFER APPLIES TO RESIDENTS OF THE U.K., EIRE AND NEW ZEALAND ONLY.

Hardy Boys® Mystery Stories in Armada

* For contractual reasons, Armada has been obliged to publish from No. 57 onwards before publishing Nos. 41–56. These missing numbers will be published as soon as possible.

The Secret of
the Old Mill

Franklin W. Dixon

Armada
An Imprint of HarperCollinsPublishers

First published in 1968 in the USA by
Grosset and Dunlap, Inc.
First published in the UK in 1972 by
William Collins Sons & Co. Ltd.
First published in Armada 1980
This impression 1993

Armada is an imprint of HarperCollins Children's Books, a
division of HarperCollins Publishers Ltd., 77–85 Fulham
Palace Road, Hammersmith, London W6 8JB

Printed and bound in Great Britain by
HarperCollins Manufacturing, Glasgow

Contents

"The Hardy Boys, so you're the snoopers we've trapped!"

A Narrow Escape

"WONDER what mystery Dad's working on now?" Joe Hardy asked.

His brother Frank looked eagerly down the platform of the Bayport railroad station. "It must be a very important case, the way Dad dashed off to Detroit. We'll know in a few minutes."

Joe looked at his watch impatiently. "Train's late."

Both boys were wondering too about a certain surprise their father had hinted might be ready for them upon his return.

Waiting with Frank and Joe for Mr Hardy's arrival was their best friend, Chet Morton. "Your dad's cases are always exciting—and dangerous," the plump, ruddy-faced boy remarked. "Do you think he'll give you a chance to help out on this one?"

"We sure hope so," Joe replied eagerly.

"Well, if I know you fellows," Chet went on, "you'll get mixed up in the mystery somehow—and so will I, sooner or later. There goes my peaceful summer vacation!"

Frank and Joe chuckled, knowing that Chet, despite his penchant for taking things easy and avoiding unnecessary risks, would stick by them through any peril.

Dark-haired, eighteen-year-old Frank, and blond, impetuous Joe, a year younger, had often assisted their detective father, Fenton Hardy, in solving baffling mysteries. There was nothing the two brothers liked more than tackling a tough case, either with their father or by themselves.

Chet gave a huge sigh and leaned against a baggage truck as though his weight were too much for him. "I sure could use something to eat," he declared. "I should have brought along some candy or peanuts."

The Hardys exchanged winks. They frequently needled their friend about his appetite, and Joe could not resist doing so now.

"What's the matter, Chet? Didn't you have lunch? Or did you forget to eat?"

The thought of this remote possibility brought a hearty laugh from Frank. Chet threw both boys a glance of mock indignation, then grinned. "Okay, okay. I'm going inside to get some candy from the machine."

As Chet went into the station, the Hardys looked across to the opposite platform where a northbound train roared in. The powerful diesel ground to a halt, sparks flashing from under the wheels. Passengers began to alight.

"Did you notice that there weren't any passengers waiting to board the train?" Frank remarked.

At that moment a man dashed up the stairs on to the platform towards the rear of the train. As the train started to move, the stranger made a leap for the last car.

"Guess he made it. That fellow's lucky," Joe commented as the train sped away. "*And* crazy!"

"You're telling me!" Chet exclaimed, as he rejoined the brothers. Munching on a chocolate bar, he added: "That same man stopped me in the station and asked me to change a twenty-dollar bill. There was a long line at the ticket window, so he didn't want to wait for change there. He grabbed the money I gave him and rushed out of the door as if the police were after him!"

"Boy!" Joe exclaimed. "You must be really loaded with money if you could change a twenty-dollar bill."

Chet blushed and tried to look as modest as he could. "Matter of fact, I do have a good bit with me," he said proudly. "I guess the man saw it when I pulled out my wallet to be sure the money was there."

"What are you going to do with all your cash?" Frank asked curiously. "Start a mint of your own?"

"Now, don't be funny, Frank Hardy," Chet retorted. "You must have noticed that for a long time I haven't been spending much. I've been saving like mad to buy a special scientific instrument. After your dad arrives, I'm going to pick it up."

"What kind of hobby are you latching on to this time, Chet?" Frank asked, grinning.

From past experience, Frank and Joe knew that their friend's interest in his new hobby would only last until another hobby captured his fancy.

"This is different," Chet insisted. "I'm going to the Scientific Specialities Store to buy a twin-lensed, high-powered microscope—and an illuminator to go with it."

"A microscope!" Joe exclaimed. "What are you

going to do with it—hunt for the answers to school exams?"

Frank joined Joe in a loud laugh, but Chet did not seem to think there was anything funny about it.

"Just you two wait," he muttered, kicking a stone that was lying on the platform. "You don't know whether or not I'll decide to be a naturalist or even a zoologist."

"Wow!" said Joe. "I can just see a sign: *Chester Morton, Big-game Naturalist*."

"Okay," Chet said. "Maybe even you two great detectives will need me to help you with some of your cases."

The conversation ended with Frank saying, "Here comes Dad's train."

The express from Detroit rolled into the station. The brothers and their friend scanned the passengers alighting. To their disappointment, Mr Hardy was not among them.

"Aren't there any other Bayport passengers?" Frank asked a conductor.

"No, sir," the trainman called out as he waved the go-ahead signal to the engineer and jumped back on to the car.

As the train pulled out, Joe said, "Dad must have been delayed at the last moment. Let's come back to the station and meet the four o'clock train."

"That's plenty of time for you fellows to go with me and pick up my microscope," said Chet.

The boys walked to Chet's jalopy, nicknamed Queen, parked in the station. The Queen had been painted a brilliant yellow, and "souped up" by Chet during one of the periods when engines were his hobby. It was a familiar and amusing sight around the streets of Bayport.

"She's not fancy, but she gets around pretty quick," Chet often maintained stoutly. "I wouldn't trade her for all the fancy cars in the showrooms."

"The petrol gauge reads 'Empty,'" Joe observed, as Chet backed the jalopy from the kerb. "How do you figure we'll make it downtown?"

Chet was unconcerned. "Oh, the tank's really half full. I'll have to fix that gauge."

The Hardys exchanged amused glances, knowing that Chet would soon be so absorbed in his microscope that he would forget to tinker with the car.

Suddenly Chet swung the Queen around in the parking area. The rough gravel caught in the tyre treads and rattled against the rear bumpers.

"Hey! What's the big rush?" Joe demanded. "We have three whole hours to get back there!"

"Who's in a hurry?" said Chet, adding proudly, "I'm not driving fast. I just wanted to find out if I changed the turning circle of the Queen by adjusting the tie rods."

"Some adjustment!" Joe grimaced. "Think we'll get to town in one piece?"

"Huh!" Chet snorted. "You don't appreciate great mechanical genius when you see it!"

In the business centre of Bayport the boys found traffic heavy. Fortunately Chet found a parking spot across the street from the Scientific Specialities Store and swung the car neatly into the space.

"See what I mean?" he asked. "Good old Queen.

And boy, I can't wait to start working with that microscope!" Chet exclaimed as the three boys got out and walked to the corner.

"All bugs beware," Joe grinned.

"You ought to be a whiz in science class next year," Frank said, while they waited for the light to change.

When it flashed green, the trio started across the street. Simultaneously a young boy on a bicycle began to ride towards them from the opposite side of the street.

The next moment a large saloon, its horn honking loudly, sped through the intersection against the red light and roared directly towards the Hardys and Chet. Instantly Frank gave Joe and Chet a tremendous push and they all leaped back to safety. To their horror, the saloon swerved and the young boy on the bicycle was directly in its path.

"Look out!" the Hardys yelled at him.

· 2 ·

Trailing a Detective

THE boy on the bicycle heard the Hardys' warning just in time and swerved away from the onrushing car. He skidded and ran up against the kerb.

The momentum carried the boy over the handlebars. He landed in a sitting position on the pavement, looking dazed.

"That driver must be out of his head!" Joe yelled, as he, Frank and Chet dashed over to the boy.

The saloon continued its erratic path, and finally, with brakes squealing and horn blaring, slammed into the kerb. It had barely missed a parked car.

By now the Hardys and Chet had reached the boy. He was still seated on the sidewalk, holding his head. "Are you all right?" Frank asked, bending down. The boy was about fourteen years old, very thin and tall for his age.

"I—I think so." A grateful look came into the boy's clear, brown eyes. "Thanks for the warning, fellows! Whew! That was close!"

Frank and Joe helped him to his feet. A crowd had gathered, and the Hardys had a hard time keeping the onlookers back. Just then the driver of the saloon made his way through the throng. He was a middle-aged man, and his face was ashen and drawn.

"I'm sorry! I'm sorry! My brakes wouldn't hold. Are you fellows all right?" The driver was frantic with worry. "It happened so fast—I—I just couldn't stop!"

"In that case, you're lucky no one was hurt," Frank said calmly.

The Hardys saw a familiar uniformed figure push through the crowd towards them.

"What's going on?" he demanded. He was Officer Roberts, a member of the local police department and an old friend of the Hardys. The driver of the car started to explain, but by this time he had become so confused that his statements were incoherent.

"What happened, Frank?" Officer Roberts asked.

Frank assured him no one was hurt and said that apparently the mishap had been entirely accidental, and the only damage was to the boy's bicycle. The front wheel spokes were bent and some of the paint was scratched off the mudguard. The car driver, somewhat calmer now, insisted upon giving the boy five dollars towards repairs.

"I'll phone for a tow truck," Joe offered, and hurried off to make the call while Officer Roberts got the traffic moving again.

After the garage truck had left with the sedan, and the crowd had dispersed, the boy with the bicycle gave a sudden gasp.

"My envelope!" he cried out. "Where is it?"

The Hardys and Chet looked round. Joe was the first to spot a large Manila envelope in the street near the kerb. He stepped out and picked it up. "Is this yours?" he asked.

"Yes! I was afraid it was lost!"

As Joe handed over the heavy sealed envelope, he noticed that it was addressed in bold printing to Mr Victor Peters, Parker Building, and had *Confidential* marked in the lower left-hand corner.

The boy smiled as he took the envelope and mounted his bicycle. "Thanks a lot for helping me, fellows. My name is Ken Blake."

The Hardys and Chet introduced themselves and asked Ken if he lived in Bayport.

"Not really," Ken answered slowly. "I have a summer job near here."

"Oh! Where are you working?" Chet asked.

Ken paused a moment before replying. "At a place outside of town," he said finally.

Although curious about Ken's apparent evasiveness, Frank changed the subject. He had been observing the bicycle with interest. Its handlebars were a different shape from most American models. The handgrips were much higher than the centre post, and the whole effect was that of a deep U.

"That's a nifty bike," he said. "What kind is it?"

Ken looked pleased. "It was made in Belgium. Rides real smooth." Then he added, "I'd better get back on the job now. I have several errands to do. So long, and thanks again."

As Ken rode off, Joe murmured, "Funny he's so secretive about where he lives and works."

Frank agreed. "I wonder why."

Chet scoffed. "There you go again, making a mystery out of it."

Frank and Joe had acquired their keen observation and interest in places and people from their father, one of the most famous investigators in the United States.

Only recently, the boys had solved *The Flickering Torch Mystery*. Shortly afterwards they had used all their ingenuity and courage to uncover a dangerous secret in the case of *The Secret of Pirates' Hill*.

"Come on, you two," Chet urged. "Let's get my microscope before anything else happens."

They had almost reached the Scientific Specialities Store when Joe grabbed his brother's arm and pointed down the street.

"Hey!" he exclaimed. "There's Oscar Smuff. What's *he* up to?"

The other boys looked and saw a short, stout man who was wearing a loud-checkered suit and a soft felt hat. Chet guffawed. "He acts as if he were stalking big game in Africa! Where's the lion?"

"I think"—Frank chuckled—"our friend is trying to shadow someone."

"If he is," Chet said, "how could anybody *not* know Oscar Smuff was following him?"

Oscar Smuff, the Hardys knew, wanted to be a member of the Bayport Police Department. He had read many books on crime detection but, though he tried hard, he was just not astute enough to do anything right. The boys had encountered him several times while working on their own cases. Usually Smuff's efforts at detection proved more of a hindrance than a help, and at times were actually laughable.

"Let's see what happens," said Joe.

In a second the boys spotted the man Oscar Smuff was tailing—a tall, trim, well-dressed stranger. He carried a suitcase and strode along as though he was going some place with a firm purpose in mind.

The boys could hardly restrain their laughter as they watched Smuff's amateurish attempts to put into action what he had read about sleuthing.

"He's as about inconspicuous as an elephant!" Chet observed.

Smuff would run a few steps ahead of the stranger, then stop at a store window and pretend to be looking at the merchandise on display. Obviously he was waiting for the man to pass him, but Smuff did not seem to care what kind of window he was looking in. Joe nudged Frank and Chet when Oscar Smuff paused before the painted-over window of a vacant store.

"Wonder what he's supposed to be looking at," Chet remarked.

Smuff hurried on, then suddenly stopped again. He took off his jacket, threw it over his arm, and put on a pair of horn-rimmed glasses.

"Get a load of his tactics now!" Joe laughed. "He's trying to change his appearance."

Frank chuckled. "Oscar's been studying about how to tail, but he needs a lot more practice."

"He probably suspects the man has contraband in his suitcase," Joe guessed, grinning.

The tall stranger suddenly turned and looked back at Smuff. The would-be detective had ducked into a doorway and was peering out like a child playing hide-and-seek. For a moment Smuff and the stranger stared at each other. The man shrugged as though puzzled about what was going on, then continued walking.

Smuff kept up his comical efforts to shadow his quarry, unaware that the boys were following him. Near the end of the block, the man turned into a small variety store and Smuff scurried in after him.

"Come on!" said Joe to Frank and Chet. "This is too good to miss."

The boys followed. Oscar Smuff was standing behind a display of large, red balloons. He was so intent on his quarry that he still did not notice the Hardys and Chet.

Frank looked around the store quickly and saw the stranger at the drug counter selecting some toothpaste. The suitcase was on the floor beside him. As they watched, the man picked up the toothpaste and his bag, and went up to the checkout counter. He took out a bill and gave it to the woman cashier.

Immediately Smuff went into action. He dashed from behind the balloons and across the front of the store. Elbowing several customers out of the way, he grasped the man by the arm and in a loud voice announced, "You're under arrest! Come with me!"

The man looked at Oscar Smuff as though he were crazy. So did the cashier. Other people quickly crowded round.

"What's the matter?" someone called out.

The Hardys and Chet hurried forward, as the man pulled his arm away from Smuff's grasp and demanded angrily, "What's the meaning of this?"

"You know very well what's the meaning of this," Smuff blustered, and grabbed the man's arm again.

"Now, miss"—Smuff turned to the cashier—"let me see the bill this man just gave you."

The woman was too surprised to refuse the request and handed the bill to the amateur detective.

Smuff took the money. The Hardys stepped up and peered over his shoulder. The bill was a five-dollar one. Suddenly the expression on Smuff's face changed to confusion and concern.

"Oh—er—a five—" he stuttered.

He dropped his hold on the man's arm and stared down at the floor. "Awfully sorry," he muttered. "It's been—a—mistake."

Both the man and the cashier looked completely bewildered. The next moment Smuff whirled and dashed from the store.

The Hardys and Chet rushed after him. They were overwhelmed with curiosity as to what Smuff thought the man had done. The boys soon overtook the would-be detective.

"What's up?" Joe demanded. "Looking for some-body suspicious?"

Oscar Smuff reddened when he realized the boys had witnessed his entire performance.

"Never mind," he said sharply. "I'll bet even you smart-aleck Hardys have made mistakes. Anyhow, this is different. I'm helping the police on a very special, very confidential case."

As he made the last statement, Smuff shrugged off his look of embarrassment and assumed an air of great importance.

"Well, I can't waste precious time gabbing with *you* three." Smuff turned and rushed off down the street.

The boys watched his bustling figure as he disappeared into the crowd. "I wonder what kind of case 'Detective' Smuff *is* working on?" Frank mused.

"I do too," Joe said, as Chet finally led the way into the Scientific Specialties Store.

Mr Reed, the shop owner, stood behind the counter. He was a plump, pleasant man with a shock of white hair that stood erect on his head.

"Have you come for your microscope, Chet?" he asked. As he spoke, the man's head bobbed up and down and his white hair waved back and forth as though blown by the wind.

"Yes, sir, Mr Reed," Chet said enthusiastically. "My friends, Frank and Joe, are looking forward to trying out the microscope just as much as I am."

Joe smiled a little sceptically, but Frank agreed with his chum. Chet pulled out his wallet and emptied it of ten- and twenty-dollar bills. "Here you are, Mr Reed. I've been saving for a long time so I could get the best."

"And the best this is." Mr Reed smiled. "I'll get the microscope you want from the stockroom." The proprietor picked up the money and disappeared into the back of the store.

While they waited, Chet pointed out the various instruments on display in the showcase. The Hardys were surprised at how much Chet had learned about microscopes and their use.

After waiting five minutes, Chet grew impatient. "Wonder what's keeping Mr Reed," he said. "I hope he has my 'scope in stock."

At that moment Mr Reed returned. There was a look of concern on his face.

"Don't tell me you haven't got the model," Chet groaned.

Mr Reed shook his head. When he spoke, his voice was solemn.

"It's not that, Chet," he said. "I'm afraid that one of the twenty-dollar bills you gave me is a counterfeit!"

·3·

An Unexpected Return

"COUNTERFEIT!" Chet burst out. "*Counterfeit!* It can't be. I just drew the money out of the bank this morning."

The Hardys, nonplussed, stared at the twenty-dollar bill Mr Reed was holding.

"I'm sorry, Chet," Mr Reed said sympathetically. "But just a few days ago all the store-keepers in town were notified by the police to be on the lookout for fake twenties. Otherwise I wouldn't have checked it. I can't understand, though, why the bank didn't detect it."

Frank's mind raced. "Wait a minute!" he exclaimed. "Chet, what about the man you gave change to at the station?"

"You're right, Frank!" Joe put in. "*He* must have passed Chet the phoney twenty!"

"You mean he gave it to me on purpose?" Chet asked indignantly.

"It's possible," Frank said. "Of course it would be pretty hard to prove whether he did it intentionally or not."

"What did the man look like?" Joe questioned Chet. "We got only a glimpse of him running for the train. He was medium height and stocky, but did you notice anything else about him?"

Chet thought for a few seconds. Then he said, "I do remember that the man had a sharp nose. But he was wearing sunglasses and a slouch hat, so I didn't notice much else."

The Hardys tried to fix a picture of the man in their minds. Meanwhile, Chet looked gloomily at the bogus bill.

"What luck!" he complained. "Here I am cheated out of twenty dollars and the microscope."

"I'm sorry, Chet," Mr Reed said. "I wish there was something I could do about it."

"Don't worry, Chet," said Joe. "You'll get the microscope anyway." He turned to his brother. "How much money do you have with you?" he asked. "I have five-fifty."

Frank emptied his pockets, but all he had was three dollars in change and bills.

"We'll lend you what we have," Joe offered. "Eight-fifty."

Although Chet protested, the Hardys insisted, and Mr Reed added, "You can take the microscope along and pay me the balance when you can."

Frank and Joe put their money on the counter, while Mr Reed went to wrap the instrument.

"Thanks. You're real pals," Chet said gratefully.

When the store owner returned with the package, Chet said, "I'll go right down to Dad's office and borrow the balance. We'll get back here later this afternoon. Thanks very much, Mr Reed."

The boys were about to leave when Frank had a sudden thought.

"Mr Reed," he said, "would you let us borrow that

counterfeit bill for some close study? We'll be sure to turn it over to Chief Collig."

"Swell idea," Joe said.

The proprietor, who was familiar with the Hardys' reputation as sleuths, readily assented. Frank put the bill in his pocket and the boys left the store.

They hurried back to Chet's car and drove to Mr Morton's real-estate office several blocks away. The office was on the ground floor of a small building. They entered and were greeted pleasantly by Mr Morton's efficient secretary, Miss Benson.

"Hello, boys. Enjoying your summer vacation?"

"Yes, thanks, Miss Benson," Chet said, eyeing his father's empty desk. "When will Dad be back?"

"Your father's gone for the day, Chet," she replied. "He decided to go home early."

"That's funny," Chet mused. "Dad usually stays until five at least."

"We have time to drive out to the farm before we meet the train," Joe said. "Let's go."

The Morton farm was on the outskirts of Bayport. When Chet swung the car into the driveway, Joe noticed with pleasure that Iola, Chet's sister, was waving to them from the front porch. Dark-haired Iola, slim and vivacious, was Joe's favourite date.

When they told her about the counterfeit bill, she exclaimed, "What a shame!"

Joe agreed emphatically. "And we'd sure like to get a lead on the man who passed it to Chet."

"Sounds as if you Hardys are in the mood for some sleuthing," Iola said, with a twinkle in her eye.

"What's this about sleuthing?" asked attractive Mrs

Morton as she came outside and joined the group.

The boys quickly explained. Then Chet asked his mother, "Is Dad around?"

Mrs Morton smiled. "He isn't here right now, Chet. He's attending to an important job."

Chet looked disappointed until his sister giggled and said, "Dad's not too far away." Iola winked at her mother and they both began to laugh.

"Your father's important job is at his favourite fishing spot," Mrs Morton told Chet.

"Fishing!" Chet exclaimed. "He never goes fishing during the week!"

"He did this time," said Mrs Morton. "I guess the good weather was too much for him to resist."

A few minutes later the boys were in the jalopy and driving down a country road bordered by woods. Half a mile farther, Chet stopped and turned off the Queen's engine. The sound of rushing water could be heard.

"This is the spot," Chet announced, and they started off through the woods.

The boys soon came to a clear, running stream and spotted Mr Morton seated contentedly on the bank. He was leaning against a tree, holding his rod lightly between his knees and steadying it with his hands.

Just as the boys called a greeting to him, the line began to jerk and almost immediately the rod bent till the tip was close to the water. Mr Morton leaped to his feet and shouted, "Just a minute, fellows! I've hooked a beauty!"

Mr Morton was an expert. He let the fish take just enough line to bury the hook properly, then he very gently braked the reel with his thumb.

So intent was Mr Morton on his fishing that he was not aware that his son was now rushing down the slope towards him. Suddenly Chet slipped on a moss-covered rock and fell forward. He lost his grip on the box containing the microscope and it flew towards the water. Joe, behind Chet, leaped forward and grabbed the box.

"Whew!" Chet exclaimed, regaining his balance. "Good work, Joe! Thanks a million!"

The three boys joined Mr Morton, who was busy landing his catch, a fine, small-mouthed black bass. He held up the fish for them to admire. "Isn't it a beauty, boys?" he said.

"Terrific, Dad," Chet replied, still out of breath from his near tumble. "And I have something to show *you*."

He unwrapped the package and held out the microscope. Mr Morton put the fish in his creel, then studied the instrument closely.

"It's a topnotch one, son," he declared. "And just the model you wanted."

"Yes, Dad. Only there's a slight problem connected with it."

"Oh—oh." Mr Morton chuckled good-naturedly. "I should have known from the look on your face. You didn't have enough money, after all. Well, how much do you need?"

"That isn't all there is to it," Chet hastened to inform him, and told about the counterfeit bill.

Mr Morton's face darkened. "I hope we're not in for a flood of phoney bills."

Frank nodded. "Especially since these are very clever imitations."

Chet's father handed over twenty dollars in small bills.

"Thanks, Dad."

"From now on, Chet, be careful about giving change to strangers," Mr Morton cautioned.

"I will," his son promised fervently. "Getting cheated once is enough!"

Chet paid the Hardys the money they had lent him. Then he said to his father, "I sure was surprised when Mother told me you were fishing—in the middle of the week."

Mr Morton smiled broadly. "I've been working hard the past year on the big sale of land to Elekton Controls," he said. "I thought it was time to take an afternoon off and do some thinking while the fish were nibbling."

"Is that the property behind the plant they just finished building?" asked Frank.

"That's right." Mr Morton pointed upstream. "You can just see the top of the main building from here."

"The property you sold has the old Turner mill on it," Joe remarked. "Quite a contrast. A company that makes top-secret control parts for space missiles in a modern building right next to an ancient, abandoned mill."

"I suppose they'll tear the old place down," Frank remarked.

"No, Elekton has decided to use it," Mr Morton went on. "I suggested to them that the old mill would make an attractive gatehouse for the plant's rear entrance. After all, it's a historic place, built by the settlers when this whole area was inhabited by Indians.

The company has renovated the old mill a bit, restoring the old living quarters and adding modern facilities."

"Is someone living there?" Joe asked with interest.

"I understand a couple of their employees are," Mr Morton replied. Then he continued, "They've even repaired the wheel, so it's turning again. Hearing the rushing water and the grinding of the wheel's gear mechanism brought back memories to me."

"About the Indians, Dad?" Chet joked.

"Not quite, son." His father smiled. "But I *can* remember when the mill produced the best flour around here. Your grandmother made many a delicious loaf of bread from wheat ground in the Turner mill."

"That's for me!" Chet said.

Everyone laughed as Mr Morton reminisced further about having seen the mill in full operation when he was a boy. Suddenly he and the Hardys noticed that Chet had fallen silent. There was a familiar, faraway look in his eyes.

Joe grinned. "Chet, you're turning some new idea over in your mind."

"That's right," Chet said excitedly. "I've been thinking that maybe I could get a summer job at Elekton."

Mr Morton exchanged amazed glances with the Hardys at the thought of Chet working during the summer vacation! But, with growing enthusiasm, Chet went on:

"I could earn the twenty dollars I owe you, Dad. Besides, if I am going to be a scientist, I couldn't think of a better place to work."

"Elekton's a fine company," his father said. "I wish you luck, son."

"Thanks, Dad." Chet smiled broadly. "See you later. I have to go now and pay Mr Reed the money I owe him."

On the drive back to town, Chet told Frank and Joe that he was going to apply for a job at the Elekton plant the next day.

"We'll go along," Joe offered. "I'd like to see the plant and the old mill."

"Swell," said Chet.

When they reached the shopping area in Bayport, Chet drove directly to Mr Reed's store. The three boys had just alighted from the parked car when Chet excitedly grabbed his friends' arms.

"There he is!" the chubby boy exclaimed. "Right down the street—the man who gave me that phoney twenty!"

·4·

The Shadowy Visitor

"There he goes! Across the street!" Joe said excitedly. "Let's ask him about the counterfeit bill!"

The three boys broke into a run, dodging in and out of the crowd of afternoon shoppers. The Hardys kept their eyes trained on the stocky figure of their quarry.

But their chase was halted at the corner by a red traffic light against them. The street was congested with vehicles and it was impossible for the boys to get across.

"What luck!" Joe growled impatiently.

It seemed to be the longest red light they had ever encountered. When it changed, the threesome streaked across the street—but it was too late. The stocky man was lost to sight. The Hardys raced down the next two blocks, peering in every direction, but to no avail.

Disappointed, Frank and Joe went back to Chet, who had stopped to catch his breath.

"We lost him," Joe reported tersely.

Frank's eyes narrowed. "I have a hunch that man who passed the bogus twenty-dollar bill to Chet knew it was counterfeit. That last-second dash for the train was just a gimmick to make a fast getaway. But his showing up here in Bayport a couple of hours after he took the train out of town is mighty peculiar."

Joe and Chet agreed. "He probably got off in Bridgeport," Frank went on. "That's the nearest big town."

As the boys walked back towards the Scientific Specialties Store, they speculated about the source of the supply of bogus money.

"Maybe it's Bridgeport," Frank said. "That could be one of the reasons he took the train there—to get a new supply, or palm off more."

"You mean they might actually make the stuff there?" Chet asked.

Frank shrugged. "Could be," he said. "I hope no more counterfeit bills are passed in Bayport."

"There probably will be," Chet said ruefully, "if this town is full of easy marks like me."

"Let's keep a sharp lookout for that fake money-passer from now on," Joe said, "and other clues to the counterfeit ring."

"Who knows," Chet put in, "it could turn out to be your next case."

As soon as Mr Reed had been paid, the boys drove to Bayport Police Headquarters. Chet decided to take his microscope into headquarters and show it to Chief Ezra Collig. The keen-eyed, robust officer was an old friend of Fenton Hardy and his sons. Many times the four had co-operated on cases.

"Sit down," the chief said cordially. "I can see that you boys have something special on your minds. Another mystery?"

He leaned forward expectantly in his chair.

"It's possible, Chief," replied Frank, as he handed over the counterfeit bill. Quickly the Hardys explained what had happened, then voiced their suspicions of the man who had just eluded them.

"Have there been any other reports of people receiving fake bills?" Joe asked the officer.

Chief Collig nodded. "Chet's not the first to be fooled," he replied. "Since the Secret Service alerted us to watch for these twenty-dollar bills, we've had nearly a dozen complaints. But we've instructed the people involved not to talk about it."

"Why?" Chet asked curiously.

"It's part of our strategy. We hope to trap at least some of the gang by lulling them into a feeling of false security."

The boys learned that Chet's description of the stocky stranger tallied with what the police had on file.

"He's a slippery one," the chief added. "It sounds to me as if the man wears a different outfit each time he shoves a bill."

"Shoves?" echoed Chet.

"A shover—or passer—is a professional term for people who pass counterfeit money," Chief Collig explained. He rubbed the bogus bill between his fingers. "This is a clever forgery," he said. "Let's see what it looks like under your microscope, Chet."

It took just a minute to rig and focus the microscope. Then, under Chief Collig's directions, the boys scrutinized the faults in the bill.

"Look at the serial number," the chief pointed out. "That's the large, coloured group of numbers that appears on the upper right and lower left portions of the bill."

As the boys peered at the number, Chief Collig made some quick calculations on his desk pad. "Divide the serial number by six," he went on, "and in this case, the remainder is two."

When the boys looked puzzled the chief smiled. "On the upper left portion of the note you'll see a small letter. One that is not followed by a number. That's the check letter, and in this case it's B."

The boys listened as Chief Collig further explained, "If the letter B corresponds to the remainder two, after you have done the division, it means the bill is either genuine—or a careful fake. The same way with the remainder, one. The check letter would be A or G; and with the remainder three, the check letter C or I, and so on."

"Wow! Some arithmetic!" Chet remarked.

Frank looked thoughtful. "In this case, the test of the divisional check indicates the bill is genuine."

"Exactly," Chief Collig said. "And the portrait of Jackson is good. The border, sometimes called lathe or scrollwork, is excellent."

"But, Chief," said Joe, puzzled, "everything you've mentioned points towards the bill's being the real thing."

"That's right. However, you'll see through the microscope that the lines in the portrait are slightly greyish and the red and blue fibres running through the bank note have been simulated with coloured ink."

In turn, the boys peered through the microscope,

observing the points the chief had called to their attention.

Chief Collig snapped off the light in Chet's microscope and pulled the bill out from under the clips that were holding it in place.

He handed the fake bill to Frank and at the same time gave him a genuine one from his wallet. "Now feel the difference in the paper quality," he directed.

Frank did so and could tell immediately that the forged bill was much rougher and thicker than the genuine one.

Just then the chief's telephone rang. He answered it, speaking quickly. When he hung up, Chief Collig said, "I must go out on a call, boys. Thanks for bringing in this bill. If you come across any others like it, or clues that might help the police, let me know. In the meantime, I'll relay your description of the suspect to the Secret Service, and also turn this bill over to them."

Chief Collig rose from his desk, and the boys walked out of the building with him. On the way, Joe said, "I wonder if Oscar Smuff has heard of the counterfeiting racket, and is—er—working on it."

"I wouldn't be surprised." The chief sighed. "That fellow will never give up."

The boys did not mention their encounter with Smuff earlier in the afternoon, but they were fairly certain that Oscar Smuff had trailed the man because he was a stranger in town and had been carrying a suitcase. The aspiring detective undoubtedly had jumped to the conclusion that the suitcase was filled with counterfeit money.

When the chief had gone, Joe glanced at his watch.

"If we're going to meet Dad's train, we'd better get started."

The three boys climbed into the jalopy and drove off. They arrived at the station just as the four o'clock train was coming to a halt.

A moment later they spotted Mr Hardy alighting from the rear car. "Dad!" cried Frank and Joe, and dashed to greet him, followed by Chet.

Fenton Hardy, a tall, distinguished-looking man, smiled broadly. "I appreciate this special reception—and a ride home too," he added, noticing Chet's jalopy.

"Right this way, sir," Chet grinned.

Joe took his father's suitcase and everyone went to the car. As they rode along, the boys gave Mr Hardy an account of the afternoon's exciting events.

The detective listened intently. In conclusion, Frank said, "Dad, does your new case have anything to do with the counterfeiting ring?"

Mr Hardy did not answer for a moment. His mind seemed to be focused on another matter. Finally he said, "No. But I'll be glad to help you boys track down any clues to these counterfeiters. I have a feeling you'll be on the lookout for them!"

"We sure will!" Joe said emphatically.

As they turned into the Hardy driveway, Frank said, "Maybe more leads will show up around here."

Fenton Hardy agreed. "That's a strong possibility."

They were met at the door by Aunt Gertrude, Mr Hardy's unmarried sister. She was a tall, angular woman, somewhat peppery in manner, but extremely kindhearted. Miss Hardy had arrived recently for one of her frequent long visits with the family. In her forth-right manner she was constantly making dire predictions about the dangers of sleuthing, and the terrible fate awaiting anyone who was a detective.

She greeted her brother affectionately as everyone went into the living-room. With a sigh she asked, "Will you be home for a while this time, Fenton, before you have to go dashing off on another case?"

Chuckling, Mr Hardy replied, "I'll probably be around for a while, Gertrude—especially if the boys run into any more counterfeit money."

"What! Laura, did you hear that?" Aunt Gertrude turned to a slim, attractive woman who had just entered the room.

"I did." Mrs Hardy greeted her husband, then urged the boys to explain.

After hearing of Chet's experience, both women shook their heads in dismay. "Well, the sooner those counterfeiters are caught, the better!" Aunt Gertrude declared firmly.

"That's what we figure, Aunty," Joe spoke up. "We'll see what we can do! Right, Frank?"

"You bet."

Chet added, grinning, "With the Hardy boys on their trail, those counterfeiters won't have a chance!"

"And Laura and I will lose sleep worrying," Aunt Gertrude prophesied.

Frank and Joe exchanged winks, knowing that actually she and Mrs Hardy were proud of the boys' sleuthing accomplishments, though sometimes fearful of the dangers they encountered.

"What delayed you today, Fenton?" Aunt Gertrude asked her brother. "Another case, I suppose."

Mr Hardy explained, "There is a special matter I'm investigating, but I'm not at liberty to talk about it yet."

His next remark diverted the boys' attention from the counterfeiters. "Frank and Joe, will you be free tomorrow to see the surprise I have for you both?" he asked. "It'll be ready late in the afternoon."

"We sure will!" his sons exclaimed together. They knew what they hoped the surprise would be, but did not dare count on it.

The brothers tried without success to coax a hint from their family.

"All I can say," Aunt Gertrude remarked, "is that you're mighty lucky boys!" With a deep sigh she added, "But this surprise certainly won't help my peace of mind!"

"Oh, Aunty!" said Joe. "You don't really worry about us, do you?"

"Oh, no!" she exploded. "Only on weekdays, Saturdays and Sundays!"

Before Chet left for home, he reminded Frank and Joe of his intention to apply to Elekton Controls Limited for a job.

Overhearing him, Mr Hardy was immediately interested. "So you want to enter the scientific field, Chet?" he said. "Good for you and lots of luck!"

The detective told the boys that the company, in addition to manufacturing controls, was engaged in secret experiments with advanced electronic controls.

"Not too long ago," he concluded, "I met some of Elekton's officers."

It flashed through Chet's mind that he might ask the detective to make an appointment for him, but he decided not to. He wanted to get the job without help from anyone. Frank and Joe suggested that Chet came for them early the next afternoon.

"I have an idea!" Chet exclaimed. "Let's go earlier and take along a picnic lunch. We'll be right near Willow River. After I apply for a job, we can eat by the water. Then you fellows can help me collect bark and stone specimens."

"Microscope study, eh?" Frank grinned. "Okay. It's a deal."

At supper Aunt Gertrude commented wryly, "There'll be two moons in the sky when Chet Morton settles down to a job!"

The others laughed, then the conversation reverted once more to counterfeiting. Mr Hardy backed up Chief Collig's statement that the bogus twenty-dollar bills being circulated were clever imitations. "I heard that the Secret Service is finding it a hard case to crack," he added.

Frank and Joe were wondering about their father's other case. They realized it must be extremely confidential, and refrained from questioning him.

In the middle of the night, Joe was suddenly awakened by a clattering sound. He leaped out of bed and rushed across the room to the front window. It was a dark, moonless night, and for a moment Joe could see nothing.

But suddenly he detected a movement near the

front door, then saw a shadowy figure running down the path to the street.

"Hey!" Joe called out. "Who are you? What do you want?"

At the end of the path the mysterious figure leaped on to a bicycle. It swerved, nearly throwing the rider, but he regained his balance and sped off into the darkness.

"What's going on?" Joe cried out.

·5·

The Bicycle Clue

JOE ran downstairs to the front door, flung it open, and dashed outside. He reached the end of the path and peered in the direction the mysterious cyclist had taken. The person was not in sight.

Puzzled, Joe walked back slowly to the house. Had the stranger come there by mistake? "If not, what did he want?" Joe wondered.

The rest of the Hardy family had been awakened by Joe's cries to the stranger. By this time they were clustered at the doorway and all the lights in the house were on.

"What's the matter, Joe?" Aunt Gertrude demanded. "Who were you calling to at this unearthly hour?"

Joe was about to reply when he noticed a large white envelope protruding from the mailbox. He pulled it out, and saw that his father's name was typed on the front. "This is for you, Dad."

Joe handed the envelope to Mr Hardy. "That fellow on the bike must have left it."

Joe was besieged with questions, and he explained what had happened.

"It's a funny way to deliver a message," Frank commented.

"Very suspicious, if you ask me!" Aunt Gertrude snapped.

Suddenly they all noticed that Mr Hardy was frowning at the contents of the envelope—a plain piece of white paper.

"What does it say, Fenton?" Mrs Hardy asked anxiously.

He read the typed message: " '*Drop case or else danger for you and family.*' "

There was silence for a moment, then Aunt Gertrude exclaimed, "I knew it! We can't get a decent night's sleep with three detectives in the family! I just *know* there's real trouble brewing!"

Although she spoke tartly, the others realized Miss Hardy was concerned, as always, for her brother's safety.

"Now, don't worry, Gertrude," Fenton Hardy said reassuringly. "The boys and I will be on guard against any danger. This note probably is the work of a harmless crank."

Aunt Gertrude tossed her head as though she did not believe this for a moment.

"Let's all look around for clues to the person on the bike," Frank suggested.

Flashlights were procured, and the entire family searched the grounds thoroughly on both sides of the front doorstoop and the walk. As Frank and his aunt neared the end of the front walk, Miss Hardy cried out, "There's something—next to that bush."

Frank picked up the object. "A bicycle pedal!" he exclaimed. "Aunty, this is a terrific clue! I think we have *four* detectives in the family!"

His aunt forced a rather embarrassed smile.

"The pedal must've fallen off the bike Joe saw," Frank said. "That's why it swerved."

Back in the house, the family gathered in the kitchen. They were too excited to go back to bed immediately, and the boys were eager to question their father. They all had biscuits and lemonade.

"What case did the warning refer to?" Joe asked.

"I can't be sure," the detective replied slowly.

Again the boys wondered about Mr Hardy's secret case, and longed to know what it involved. "Maybe the threat is connected with that one," Frank thought. Before the boys went to sleep, they decided to track down the pedal clue early the next morning.

Right after breakfast, Chet telephoned. He told Frank, who took the call, that his sister Iola and her friend Callie Shaw had offered to pack lunch if they could go along on the picnic.

"Swell," Frank said enthusiastically. Callie was his favourite date. "In the meantime, how'd you like to do some sleuthing with us?"

"Sure! What's up?"

Frank quickly told Chet about the excitement of the previous night. "Meet us here as soon as you can."

When Frank and Joe informed Mr Hardy of their plan to trace the pedal, he nodded approval. "I must go out of town for a short while," he said. "But first, I'd like to examine the warning note in the lab."

The boys went with him to their fully-equipped laboratory over the garage. Mr Hardy dusted the note carefully, but when he blew the powder away, there was no sign of a fingerprint.

Holding the note up to the light, Mr Hardy said, "There's no watermark. Of course, this is not a full sheet of paper."

"Dead end, so far." Joe frowned. "If we could only locate the typewriter this message was written on—"

Shortly after Mr Hardy had driven off in his saloon, Chet arrived. "Where to, fellows?" he asked as they set off in the Queen.

"Centre of town," Joe replied.

On the way, the brothers briefed Chet on their plan, which was to make inquiries at all the bicycle supply stores. In the first four they visited, Frank showed the pedal and asked if there had been any requests for a replacement that morning. All the answers were negative. Finally, at the largest supply store in Bayport, they obtained some helpful information.

"This particular pedal comes from a bike made in Belgium," the proprietor said. "There isn't a store in town that carries parts for it."

The boys were disappointed. As Frank put the pedal back in his pocket he asked the proprietor where parts for the Belgian bicycle could be purchased.

"It might be worth your while to check over in Bridgeport," the man said. "I think you'll find Traylor's handles them."

"It's an odd coincidence," Frank remarked, when the boys were back in the car. "We've come across two Belgian bikes in two days."

When they reached the Traylor store in Bridgeport, the young detectives learned they had just missed a customer who had purchased a pedal for a Belgian bike.

"Who was he?" Frank inquired.

"I don't know."

"What did he look like?" Joe asked.

The proprietor's brow wrinkled. "Sorry. I was too busy to pay much attention, so I can't tell you much. As far as I can remember, he was a tall boy, maybe about fourteen."

The three friends knew this vague description was almost useless. There probably were hundreds of boys living in the surrounding area who fitted that description.

As the boys reached the street, Joe said determinedly, "We're not giving up!"

"Hey!" Chet reminded his friends. "It's almost time to pick up the girls."

Within an hour the five young people were turning off the highway on to a side road parallel to Elekton's east fence. A little farther on, Chet made a right turn and followed the dirt road that led to the rear entrance of the plant.

"Any luck sleuthing?" Pretty, brown-eyed Callie Shaw asked the Hardys.

"What makes you think we were sleuthing?"

"Oh, I can tell!" Callie said, her eyes twinkling. "You two always have that detective gleam in your eyes when you're mixed up in a mystery!"

"They certainly have!" Iola agreed, laughing.

When they reached a grove bordering Willow River, which was to their left, Chet pulled over. "I'll park here."

The girls had decided they would like to see the changes which had been made in the old mill. As the group approached Elekton's gatehouse, they were amazed at the transformation.

No longer did the mill look shabby and neglected. The three-storey structure had been completely re-painted and the weeds and overgrowth of years cleared away. The grounds and shrubbery of the whole area were neatly trimmed.

"Look!" said Frank. "There's the mill wheel!"

As the Hardys and their friends watched the huge wheel turning, they felt for a moment that they were living in olden days. Water which poured from a pond over a high stone dam on the south side and through an elevated millrace caused the wheel to revolve.

"Oh!" Callie exclaimed admiringly as she spotted a little bridge over the stream from the falls. "It looks just like a painting!"

About three hundred yards from the north side of the mill was the closed rear gate of Elekton's ultra-modern plant.

"Some contrast between the old and the new!" Joe remarked, as they left the dirt road and walked up the front path to the gatehouse.

Suddenly the door opened and a dark-haired, muscular man in uniform came out to meet them. "What can I do for you?" he asked. "I'm the gate guard here."

"I'd like to apply for a summer job at Elekton," Chet told him.

"Have you an appointment?"

"No," replied Chet. "I guess I should have phoned first."

The guard agreed. "You would've saved yourself time and trouble," he said. "I'm sure there aren't any openings, especially for temporary help."

"Well, couldn't I go in and leave an application with the personnel manager?" Chet asked.

The guard shrugged. "Tell you what—I'll phone the personnel office instead," he offered, and went back into the mill.

While they waited, the five looked around. At the south side of the mill grounds, a slender, greying man who wore overalls was clipping the low hedges.

"Look, Callie," said Iola, pointing towards a spot near the hedges. "Isn't that quaint? An old flour barrel with ivy growing out of it!"

"Charming." Callie smiled.

The girls and boys started over towards the mill for a closer inspection. At that same moment the guard came to the door. "Just as I told you," he called out to Chet. "No openings! Sorry!"

"Too bad, Chet," Joe said sympathetically. "Well, at least you can keep on relaxing."

Despite his disappointment, Chet grinned. "Right now I'm starved. Let's go down to the river and have our picnic."

He thanked the guard, and the young people started to walk away. Suddenly Frank stopped and looked back at the mill. Propped against the south wall was a bicycle. Quickly he ran over to examine it. "This looks like a Belgian model," Frank thought. "Sure is," he told himself. "The same type Ken Blake has."

On impulse, Frank pulled the pedal from his pocket and compared it to those on the bike. They matched exactly. Frank noticed that one of the pedals looked much less worn than the other. "As if it had been replaced recently," he reflected, wondering excitedly if someone had used this bicycle to deliver the warning note.

"And could this bike be Ken's?" the young detective asked himself.

He inspected the front-wheel spokes. None was twisted, but several had slight dents. "They could've been straightened out easily," Frank reasoned, "and the paint scratches on the mudguard touched up."

He felt his heart beat faster as he waved his companions to join him. When Frank pointed out the clues to his brother, Joe agreed immediately.

"It could be the bicycle which was used to deliver the message—"

Joe was interrupted by a strange voice behind them. "Pardon me, but why are you so interested in that bike?"

Frank quickly slipped the pedal into his pocket as the group swung round to face the speaker. He was the man who had been clipping the hedges.

"Because just yesterday we met a boy, Ken Blake, who was riding a bike of the same model. We don't often see this Belgian make around."

For a moment the man looked surprised, then smiled. "Of course! Ken works here—does odd jobs for us around the mill. You must be the boys he met yesterday when he was delivering some copy to the printer."

"Yes," Frank replied. "When we asked Ken about his job he was very secretive."

"Well," the maintenance man said, "he has to be! This plant is doing top-secret work. All of us have been impressed with the necessity of not talking about Elekton at all."

"Is Ken around?" Joe asked nonchalantly. "We'd like to say hello."

"I'm afraid not," was the reply. "We sent him by bus this afternoon to do an errand. He won't be back until later." The man excused himself and resumed his clipping.

"We'd better eat," Iola giggled. "My poor brother is suffering."

"I sure am!" Chet rolled his eyes. Laughing, the picnickers started off.

Joe, who was in the rear, happened to glance up at the front of the mill. He was startled to catch a glimpse of a face at one of the second-storey windows. He stopped in his tracks.

"Ken Blake!" Joe said to himself.

As the young sleuth stared, mystified, the face disappeared from the window.

· 6 ·

A Mysterious Tunnel

PUZZLED, Joe continued looking up at the window of the old mill.

"What's the matter?" Iola asked him. "Did you see a ghost?"

In a low whisper, Joe explained about the face which had disappeared. "I'm sure it was Ken Blake I saw at that window!"

The others followed his gaze. "No one's there now," Iola said. "Of course the glass in all the windows is old and wavy. The sunlight on them could cause an illusion."

Chet agreed. "How could Ken be here if he was sent on an errand?"

Joe stood for a minute, deep in thought. "I can't figure it out, but I'm sure that it was no illusion. Come on, Frank. Let's check."

While the others walked down the hill, the Hardys strode up to the maintenance man, who was still trimming hedges.

"Are you sure Ken went into town?" Joe asked. "Just now I thought I saw him looking out of a second-floor window."

"You couldn't have. You must have been dreaming."
The man gave a jovial laugh.

Joe was still not convinced. Impulsively he asked,
"Does Ken ever run any errands for you at night?"

"No," the man answered readily. "He leaves his bike
here and walks home when we close at five-thirty."

"Does anyone else have access to the bike after that?"
Frank queried.

"It's kept in an open storage area under the rear of
the mill and could be taken from there easily."

Although obviously curious, the man did not ask the
Hardys the reason for their questions. He looked at his
watch.

"Excuse me, boys, I'm late for lunch." He turned
and hurried into the mill.

As the brothers hastened to catch up with Chet and
the girls, Frank said, "Another thing which makes me
wonder if that bicycle is connected with the warning
is the description of the boy who bought the pedal. *He*
could be Ken Blake."

"I agree," Joe said. "I'd sure like to question Ken."

"We'll come back another time," Frank proposed.

The group picked up the picnic hamper from the
Queen and strolled down a narrow path through the
woods leading to Willow River.

"Here's a good spot." Callie pointed to a shaded level
area along the bank. "We haven't been in this section
before."

Soon everyone was enjoying the delicious lunch the
girls had prepared: chicken sandwiches, potato salad,
chocolate cake, and lemonade. While they were eating,
the girls were the targets of good-natured kidding.

"Boy!" Joe exclaimed, as he finished his piece of cake. "This is almost as good as my mother and Aunt Gertrude make."

"*That's* a compliment!" Chet said emphatically.

Callie's eyes twinkled. "I know it is. Joe's mother and aunt are the best cooks ever!"

Iola sniffed. "I don't know about this compliment stuff. There's something on your mind, Joe Hardy!"

Joe grinned. "How are you on apple pie and cream puffs and—?"

"Oh, stop it!" Iola commanded. "Otherwise you won't get a second piece of cake!"

"I give up." Joe handed over his paper plate.

After lunch everyone but Chet was ready to relax in the sun. Normally he was first the one to suggest a period of rest, even a nap, but now his new project was uppermost in his mind.

"Let's start to collect the specimens for my microscope," he urged his friends.

The Hardys groaned good-naturedly at Chet's enthusiasm, but readily agreed.

"We'll need some exercise to work off that meal." Frank grinned.

The girls packed the food wrappings in the hamper. Then, single file, the group walked downstream, paying careful attention to the rocks and vegetation. Chet picked up several rocks and leaves, but discarded them as being too common.

"Are you looking for something from the Stone Age?" Joe quipped. "Maybe a prehistoric fossil?"

"Wouldn't you be surprised if I found one?" Chet retorted.

They followed a bend in the river and came to a small cove with a rocky, shelving beach. Here the willow trees did not grow so thickly. The shoreline curved gently round to the right before it came to a halt in a sandy strip along the river bank.

"What a nice spot," said Callie. "We'll have to come here again and wear our swim suits."

"Look!" cried Iola. "What's that?"

She pointed to a dark opening beneath a rocky ledge which bordered the beach.

"A cave!" exclaimed Joe and Frank together.

Intrigued, the five hurried along the beach for a closer look. Eagerly the Hardys and Chet peered inside the entrance. The interior was damp, and the cave's walls were covered with green growth.

"This'll be a perfect spot to look for specimens," Chet said. "Let's go in!"

The boys entered the cave. The girls, however, decided to stay outside.

"Too spooky—and crowded!" Callie declared. "Iola and I will sun ourselves while you boys explore."

The Hardys and Chet could just about stand up in the low-ceilinged cave. Frank turned on his pocket flashlight and pointed to an unusual yellow-green fungus on the right side of the cave. "Here's a good sample of lichens, Chet."

Soon the boys were busy scraping various lichens off the rocks. Gradually they moved deeper into the cave. Frank halted in front of a pile of rocks at the rear.

"There ought to be some interesting specimens behind these stones," he said. "They look loose enough to move."

Together, the three boys rolled some of the rocks to one side. To their great surprise, the stones concealed another dark hole.

"Hey! This looks like a tunnel!"

Excitedly, Joe poked his flashlight into the opening. By its beam they could see that the hole appeared to extend into the side of the bank.

"Let's go in and see where the tunnel goes!" Joe urged.

"Okay," Frank agreed eagerly. "We'll have to move more of these rocks before we can climb through. I wonder who put them here and why."

Rapidly the boys pushed rocks aside until the narrow tunnel entrance was completely exposed. Joe crawled in first, then Frank.

Chet tried to squeeze his bulky form through the space but quickly backed out. "It's too tight for me," he groaned. "I'll stay here and collect more specimens. Anyhow, I'll bet some animal made the tunnel and it doesn't lead anywhere."

"I'm sure no animal did this," Joe called back, aiming his flashlight at the earthen walls of the tunnel. "Look how hard-packed the sides are—as if dug out by a shovel."

Frank was of the same opinion. He pointed to rough-hewn wooden stakes placed at intervals along the sides and across the ceiling. "I wonder who put those supports here—and when."

The Hardys crawled ahead carefully. There was just room in the passageway for a normal-sized person to get through.

Presently Joe called back to his brother, "Look

ahead! I can see a sharp bend to the right. Let's keep going."

Frank was about to reply when the brothers were startled by a girl's scream from outside.

"That's Callie!" Frank exclaimed. "Something's wrong!"

Sleuthing by Microscope

FRANK and Joe scrambled through the tunnel and out of the cave. They found Chet and the girls staring at an arrow embedded in the sandy beach.

"It—it almost hit us," Iola quavered. Callie, who was white-faced with fear, nodded.

Joe was furious. "Whoever shot it shouldn't be allowed to use such a dangerous weapon!" he burst out. "That's a hunting arrow—it could have caused serious injury."

Chet gulped. "M-maybe the Indians haven't left here after all," he said, trying to hide his nervousness.

Joe turned to dash off into the woods to search for the bowman.

"Wait!" Frank called. He had pulled the arrow from the sand. "This was done deliberately," he announced grimly, holding the arrow up for all of them to see. Attached to the shaft just below the feathers was a tiny piece of paper. It had been fastened on with adhesive tape.

Frank unrolled the paper and read the printed message aloud: " *'Danger. Hardys beware.'* "

Chet and the girls shuddered and looked around fearfully, as though they expected to see the bowman behind them.

"You boys *are* involved in a new mystery!" Callie exclaimed. "Your own or your father's?"

Frank and Joe exchanged glances. It certainly seemed as though they were involved, but they had no way of knowing *which* case. Did it involve the counterfeit money? Or was it the case their father could not divulge?

"A warning did come to Dad," Frank admitted. "This one obviously was meant for Joe and me. Whoever shot the arrow trailed us here."

Joe frowned. "I wonder if the same person sent both warnings."

"I still think Ken Blake could give us a clue," Frank said. "But we must remember that anybody could have taken the bike from the storage place under the mill."

Frank pocketed the latest warning, then the five searched quickly for any lead to the bowman. They found none. When the group returned to the beach, Joe looked at the sky. "We're in for a storm—and not one of us has a raincoat."

The bright summer sun had disappeared behind towering banks of cumulus clouds. There were rumbles of heavy thunder, followed by vivid flashes of lightning. The air had become humid and oppressive.

"Let's get out of here!" Chet urged. "This isn't a picnic any more!"

The young people hastened through the woods and up the road to Chet's jalopy. As they drove off, rain began coming down in torrents. The sky grew blacker.

Callie shivered. "It seems so sinister—after that awful arrow."

Chet dropped his sister off at the Morton farm and

at the same time picked up his new microscope. He begged to try out the instrument on both warning notes and the Hardys smilingly agreed, although they had an up-to-date model of their own.

By the time they had said goodbye to Callie at her house, and Chet had driven the Queen into the Hardys' driveway, the storm had ended. The sun shone brightly again.

Immediately the three boys went to the laboratory over the garage. Here Frank carefully dusted the arrow and the second warning note for prints. He blew the powder away, and Joe and Chet looked over his shoulder as he peered through the magnifying glass.

"Nothing. Same as the warning to Dad. The person no doubt wore gloves."

"Now to compare this paper with the first note," Joe said.

"Right," his brother agreed. "You have the combination to the cabinet in Dad's study. Chet and I will rig up the microscope while you get the note from the file."

Frank and Chet focused and adjusted the microscope, making sure it was level on the table. They plugged in the illuminator and checked to see that it did not provide too dazzling a reflection. When Joe returned, Chet took the two pieces of paper and fitted them side by side under the clips on the base.

"Okay. Want to take a look, fellows?"

Frank, then Joe, studied both papers. "The quality and texture are definitely the same," Frank observed.

Next, he lifted the second note from under the clips

and slowly moved the paper back and forth under the lenses.

"A watermark!" he exclaimed, stepping back so that the others could look at the faint imprint.

"Sure is!" said Joe. "A five-pointed star. This could be a valuable clue! We can try to track down exactly where this paper came from."

"And also the arrow," said Chet. "I'll make the rounds of sports stores in town."

"Swell, Chet. Thanks," Frank said.

After their friend had left, the Hardys consulted the classified directory for paper manufacturers.

They made several calls without any luck. Finally they learned that the Quality Paper Company in Bridgeport manufactured paper bearing the five-pointed star watermark. The brothers wanted to go at once to get more information, but realized this errand would have to wait.

"Dad will be home soon," Frank reminded his brother. "We don't want to miss our surprise!"

"Right. And I'd like to tell him about the warning on the arrow."

When Chet returned from a round of the sports shops, he was glum. "I wasn't much help," he said. "The arrow isn't new, and all the stores I checked told me it was a standard model that could be purchased at any sports shop in the country."

"Never mind, Chet," said Frank. "At least giving your microscope a trial run helped us to spot the watermark on the second warning note. We've located a company that manufactures paper with the star watermark."

Chet's face brightened. "Let me know if you find out

anything else," he said, packing up his microscope. "I guess I'll take off—and do some nature study for a change."

After he had driven off, Frank and Joe walked to the house. Their minds once more turned to the surprise Mr Hardy had for them.

"Wouldn't it be terrific if—" Joe said to Frank excitedly. "Do you think it *is*?"

"I'm just hoping." Frank grinned.

Just then a newsboy delivered the evening newspaper. The brothers entered the house and went into the living-room. Frank scanned the front page and pointed out an item about new trouble in an Indiana electronics plant.

"That's where an explosion took place a couple of months ago," Joe remarked. "Sabotage, the investigators decided."

"And before that," Frank added, "the same thing happened at a rocket research lab in California. Another unsolved case."

"Seems almost like a chain reaction," Frank remarked.

Any mystery appealed to the boys, but they did not have much chance to discuss this one. The telephone rang. Aunt Gertrude, after taking the call, burst into the living-room. From the look on her face, Frank and Joe could tell she was indignant, and at the same time frightened.

"What's the matter, Aunty?" Joe asked.

"More threats—that's all!" she cried out. "This time by telephone. A man's voice—he sounded sinister—horrible!"

Mrs Hardy came into the living-room at that moment. "What did he say, Gertrude?" she asked.

Aunt Gertrude took a deep breath in an effort to calm down. " '*Hardy and his sons are playing with fire,*' the man said. '*They'll get burned if they don't lay off this case.*' " Miss Hardy sniffed. "I don't know what case he meant. What kind of danger *are* you boys mixed up in now?"

Frank and Joe smiled wryly. "Aunt Gertrude," Frank replied, "we really don't know. But please try not to worry," he begged her and his mother. "You know that Dad and the two of us will be careful."

When Mr Hardy came home a little later, his family told him about the threatening telephone call. The boys, however, did not mention the arrow warning in the presence of their mother and Aunt Gertrude. They knew it would only add to their concern.

Mr Hardy was as puzzled as his sons. "It's a funny thing," he said. "At this point it's impossible to tell which 'case' the person is referring to. If I knew, it might shed light on either one."

The detective grinned and changed the subject. "Right now, I want you all to come for a drive and have a look at the boys' surprise."

"Swell!" Frank and Joe exclaimed in unison.

While Aunt Gertrude and Mrs Hardy were getting ready, Frank and Joe went out to the car with their father. Quickly the boys related their afternoon's experience, concluding with the arrow incident.

The detective looked grim. "Whoever is responsible for these warnings is certainly keeping close tabs on us."

Mr Hardy and his sons speculated for a few minutes

on the fact that the pedal found in front of the house apparently had belonged to Ken's bike.

"I think Joe and I should go back tonight to the place where we had the picnic," Frank told his father. "In the darkness we'll have a better chance to sleuth without being seen. And there might be some clue we missed this afternoon."

"I suppose you're right," agreed his father. "But be cautious."

As Aunt Gertrude and Mrs Hardy came out of the house, conversation about the mystery ceased. Everyone climbed into the saloon and Mr Hardy drove off. Frank and Joe, seated alongside him, were in a state of rising suspense. Was the surprise the one thing they wanted most of all?

·8·

The Strange Mill Wheel

A FEW minutes later Mr Hardy was driving along the Bayport waterfront.

"Is the surprise here, Dad?" Joe asked excitedly.

"That's right."

Mr Hardy drove to a boathouse at the far end of the dock area and parked. He then invited the others to follow him. He walked to the door of a boathouse and unfastened the padlock.

Frank and Joe held their breaths as Mr Hardy swung back the door. For a moment they stared inside, speechless with delight. Finally Joe burst out, "Exactly what we had hoped for, Dad!" and put an arm affectionately around his father.

"What a beauty!" Frank exclaimed, and wrung Mr Hardy's hand.

Rocking between the piles lay a sleek, completely equipped motorboat. It nudged gently against clean white fenders as the waves from the bay worked their way under the boathouse door.

The boys' mother exclaimed in delight, and even Aunt Gertrude was duly impressed by the handsome craft.

"This is the same model we saw at the boat show," Joe said admiringly. "I never thought we'd own one."

"She even has the name we picked out," Frank observed excitedly. "The *Sleuth*!"

Shiny brass letters were fitted on the bow of the boat, with the port of registry, Bayport, underneath them.

Mr Hardy and his wife beamed as their sons walked up and down, praising every detail of the graceful new craft. It could seat six people comfortably. The polished fore and aft decks carried gleaming anchor fittings, and the rubbing strakes were painted white. The *Sleuth* seemed to be waiting to be taken for a run!

"May we try her out now, Dad?" Joe asked.

"Of course. She's fuelled up."

Aunt Gertrude shook her head. "The *Sleuth*'s an attractive boat, all right. But don't you two start doing any crazy stunts in it," she cautioned her nephews. "And be back for supper."

When the adults had left, Frank and Joe climbed aboard and soon had the *Sleuth* gliding into the bay. The boys had no difficulty operating the motorboat. They had gained experience running their friend, Tony Prito's boat, the *Napoli*, which had similar controls.

Taking turns at the wheel, the brothers ran the boat up and down the bay. "Terrific!" Joe shouted.

Frank grinned. "Am I glad we stuck to our agreement with Dad, and saved up to help buy this!"

For some time the boys had been putting money towards a boat of their own into a special bank account. Mr Hardy had promised that when the account reached a certain sum, he would make up the necessary balance.

Now, as the *Sleuth* knifed through the water, Frank and Joe admired the way the stern sat down in the water when the boat gathered speed. Joe was impressed with the turning circle and the fact that no matter how sharp the twist, none of the spume sprayed into the cockpit.

"Wait until Tony and Chet see this!" Joe exclaimed, when they were pulling back towards the boathouse.

"Speaking of Tony—there he is," Frank said. Their dark-haired classmate was standing on the dock, shouting and waving to them.

Joe, who was at the wheel, brought the *Sleuth* neatly alongside. He turned off the engine as Tony rushed up.

"Don't tell me this dreamboat is yours?" he demanded in amazement.

"Nothing but," Joe said proudly.

Tony and the brothers inspected the boat carefully, comparing her various features with the *Napoli*. They lifted the battens from the *Sleuth*'s cowling and admired the powerful motor underneath.

"She's neat all right," said Tony. "But I'll still promise you a stiff race in the *Napoli*!"

"We'll take you up on it after the *Sleuth*'s broken in," Joe returned, laughing.

Tony became serious. "Say, fellows, something happened today in connection with my dad's business that I want to tell you about. Your mother said you were down here," he explained.

"What's up?" Frank asked.

Tony's father was a building contractor and also had

a construction supply yard where Tony worked during the summer. "Today I went to the bank, just before it closed, to deposit the cash and cheques we took in this week," he said. "The teller discovered that one of the bills was a counterfeit!"

"A twenty-dollar bill?" Frank guessed.

"Yes. How'd you know?"

The Hardys related Chet's experience. Tony's dark brows drew together. "I'd like to get my hands on the guy making the stuff!" he said angrily.

"So would we!" Joe stated.

The Hardys learned that the head teller had told Tony he would make a report to the Bayport police and turn the bill over to the Secret Service. "Did he explain how he could tell that the bill was a fake?" Frank asked.

"Yes," replied Tony, and from his description the Hardys were sure that the bill had come from the same batch as the one passed to Chet.

"Think back, Tony," Frank urged. "Have you any idea who gave it to you—or your father?"

Tony looked doubtful. "Three days' trade—pretty hard to remember. Of course, we know most of the customers. I did ask Mike, our yardman, who helps with sales. He mentioned one purchaser he didn't know."

Frank, eager for any possible lead, carefully questioned Tony. The Hardys learned that three days before, just at closing time, a faded green truck had driven into the Prito supply yard. "Mike remembers there were no markings on the truck—as if the name might have been painted out."

"Who was in it?" Joe prompted.

"A young boy—about fourteen—was with the driver. Mike says they bought about fifty dollars' worth of old bricks and lumber. The boy paid him in assorted bills. One was a twenty. Our other cash customers had given smaller bills."

"What did the driver look like?" Frank probed.

"Mike said he didn't notice—the fellow stayed behind the wheel. There was a last-minute rush at the yard, so the boy and Mike piled the stuff into the back of the truck. Then the driver gave the boy money to pay the bill."

Frank and Joe wondered the same thing. Had the man driving the truck passed the bogus bill deliberately? If so, was he the one who had fooled Chet? "It seems funny he'd go to so much trouble to dump one phoney twenty-dollar bill," Joe said.

Frank agreed, and added, "Besides, what would a person in league with counterfeiters want with a pile of old bricks and lumber?"

He turned to Tony. "Did Mike notice anything in particular about the boy?"

"He was tall and thin. Mike thinks he was wearing a striped shirt."

Frank and Joe exchanged glances. "Could be Ken Blake!" Joe declared. Briefly, the Hardys explained their first encounter with the boy.

"He might have been helping pick up the load for Elekton," Frank reasoned. "But why would a modern plant want second-hand building material? And why wouldn't they have the purchase billed to them?"

"What's more," his brother put in, "why didn't the

driver get out and help with the loading? Unless, perhaps, he wanted to stay out of sight as much as possible."

"Too bad Mike didn't notice the truck's licence number," Tony said. "Naturally he had no reason to at the time."

"Was there anything unusual about the truck besides the fact it wasn't marked?" Frank asked his chum.

Tony thought for a moment. "Mike did say there was a bike in the back. He had to move it out of the way."

"Ken rides one," Joe remarked.

"Well, Dad will be glad if you two pick up any clues to these counterfeiters," Tony said. "He's hopping mad at being cheated, and Mike feels sore about it."

"We'll keep our eyes open for that green truck," Frank assured him. "The whole business sounds suspicious—though the bill could have been passed accidentally."

"Let's question Ken Blake," Joe proposed.

He and his brother housed the *Sleuth*, and the three boys started homeward. On the way they continued to speculate on the counterfeiting racket.

"Let me know if I can help you detectives," Tony said, as he turned into his street.

"Will do."

That evening, when it grew dark, Frank and Joe told their mother and aunt that they were going out to do some investigating. Before they left, the boys had a chance to speak to their father in private about Tony's report of the counterfeit bill and green truck and their own hunches.

Mr Hardy agreed that the purchase of lumber and bricks seemed odd, but he felt that until more positive evidence could be obtained, it was best not to approach Elekton officials on the matter.

"I guess you're right, Dad," said Frank. "We might be way off base."

The detective wished them luck on their sleuthing mission. The boys decided to make the trip in the *Sleuth*. They rode their motorcycles down to the boat-house, parked them, then climbed aboard the new boat. Joe took the wheel and soon the sleek craft was cutting across the bay towards the mouth of Willow River.

When they entered it, Joe throttled down and carefully navigated the stream. Meanwhile, Frank shone his flashlight on the wooded banks.

"There's the cave—ahead!" he whispered.

Joe ran the boat astern a few yards and Frank dropped anchor. The brothers waded ashore, carrying their shoes and socks.

When they reached the mouth of the cave, Joe said, "Let's investigate this place first."

They went into the cave and moved forward to the tunnel. One glance told them that the tunnel had become impassable—it was filled with water.

"Must have been the cloudburst," said Frank, as they emerged from the cave. "We'll have to wait until the ground dries out. At least we can take a look through the woods and the area around the mill for clues to the bowman."

Shielding the lenses of their flashlights, so that the light beams would not be easily detected by anyone lurking in the vicinity, the boys began a thorough search of the wooded section. As they worked their way noiselessly uphill among the trees, the only sound was the eerie rattling the wind made in the leaves and branches.

Frank and Joe shone their lights beneath shrubs and rocks, and even crawled under some fallen trees. They found nothing suspicious. They were approaching the edge of the woods and could see the outline of the mill beyond. The old wheel creaked and rumbled.

Suddenly Frank whispered hoarsely, "Look! Here's something!"

Joe joined his brother, and together they examined the leather object Frank had picked up.

"An archer's finger guard," he said.

"It may be a valuable clue to the arrow warning," Joe said, as Frank pocketed the guard. "Let's go up to the mill," he proposed. "Maybe the men there have seen something suspicious."

As the boys crossed the clearing towards the gate-house, they saw that it was in darkness.

"Probably everyone has gone to bed," Frank remarked.

For a moment the brothers stood wondering what to do next. "Something's missing," Joe said, in a puzzled voice. "I have it! The mill wheel has stopped turning."

"Maybe it was switched off for the night," Frank observed.

The boys were eager to question the occupants, but decided not to awaken them.

"Let's walk round the mill," said Frank, "and look through the woods on the other side."

The boys had just passed the north corner of the

building when, with a creaking groan, the wheel started to turn again.

"There must be something wrong with the mechanism," Frank deduced. "The wheel hasn't been used for so many years that adapting it to work the generator may have put a strain on it."

"We'd better let the men know it's acting up," Joe said.

The boys retraced their steps to the mill door. As they reached it, the wheel stopped turning.

Frank and Joe stood staring off to their left where the mass of the motionless wheel was outlined against the night sky.

"Spooky, isn't it?" Joe commented.

Frank nodded, and knocked on the door. There was no response. After a short wait, he knocked again—louder this time. The sound echoed in the deep silence of the night. Still no one answered.

The Hardys waited a little longer. Finally they turned away. "Must be sound sleepers," Joe commented. "Well, maybe they'll discover what's wrong tomorrow."

Frank and Joe were about to resume their search for clues when they heard a loud crashing noise from the woods which bordered Willow River.

The boys dashed ahead to investigate. Entering the woods, they made their way stealthily forward, flashlights turned off. Silently they drew near the river.

After a few minutes they stopped and listened intently. The sound was not repeated.

"Must have been an animal," Joe whispered.

Just then they heard a rustling sound behind them

and turned to look. The next instant each received a terrific blow on the back of the head. Both boys blacked out.

· 9 ·

Tracing a Slugger

WHEN Frank regained consciousness, his first thought was of his brother. He turned his throbbing head and saw that Joe was lying next to him.

"Joe!" he exclaimed anxiously.

To his relief, Joe stirred and mumbled, "W-what happened?"

"Someone conked us on the head—"

Frank broke off as he became aware of a gentle rocking motion. He sat up. Was he still dizzy or were they moving? When his mind and vision cleared, he knew they were certainly moving.

"Hey!" he said. "We're on the *Sleuth*!"

Astonished, Joe raised himself and looked around. They were indeed aboard their boat—lying on the foredeck and slowly drifting down Willow River towards the bay. The anchor lay beside them.

"A fog's rolling in," Frank said uneasily, observing white swirls of mist ahead. "Let's start 'er up before visibility gets worse."

The boys wriggled into the cockpit and Joe pressed the starter. It would not catch. While Joe stayed at the controls, Frank climbed to the foredeck and lifted the cowling from the engine. He quickly checked to see if the distributor wires were in place. They were. There did not seem to be anything visibly wrong with the engine, but when he lifted the top off the carburettor, he found it empty.

A quick check on the petrol tank revealed the cause of the trouble. The tank had been drained.

"Fine mess we're in," he mumbled. "What was the idea?"

"The man who hit us on the head can answer that one," Joe said bitterly. "He sure did a complete job—even took both our oars!"

"We'll have to tow her," Frank said tersely, "to make more speed and guide her."

While Joe stripped to his shorts, Frank quickly led a painter through one of the foredeck fairleads.

"Take this painter," Frank said, handing Joe the rope. "Make it fast round your shoulder and swim straight ahead. I'll unhinge one of the battens and use it as a paddle and try to keep her straight. In a few minutes I'll change places with you."

The Hardys knew that keeping a dead weight like the *Sleuth* moving in a straight line would be a tough job. However, with Joe swimming ahead and Frank wielding the batten, they managed to make fairly steady progress.

It was slow, back-breaking work, and before they reached the bay, the boys had changed places three times. Their heads were pounding more than ever from the physical strain. Also, the fog had grown so dense that it was impossible to see very far ahead.

Frank, who was taking his turn in the water, did

not know how much longer he could go on.

Suddenly Joe shouted from the boat, "There's a light! Help! Help! Ahoy! Over here!" he directed at the top of his lungs.

Gradually the light approached them. Frank clambered back into the *Sleuth* as a Harbour Police boat, making its scheduled rounds, pulled alongside.

"You're just in time!" Frank gasped to the sergeant in charge. "We're exhausted."

"I can see that. You run out of petrol?" the police officer asked.

"Worse than that. Foul play," Frank replied.

"Tough luck," the sergeant said. "You can tell your story when we get to town."

The officer gave orders to his crew, and a tow-line was put on the *Sleuth*. The boys were given blankets to throw round themselves.

When the two crafts reached the Harbour Police pier, the boys went inside and gave a full account of what had happened to them and asked that the report be relayed to Chief Collig.

"We'll give you some petrol," said the sergeant who had rescued the boys. "Then do you think you can make it home alone?"

"Yes, thank you."

A half-hour later the boys, tired and disappointed, cycled home. Their mother and aunt gasped with dismay at the sight of the weary boys in the water-sodden clothing. Joe and Frank, however, made light of the evening's experience.

"We ran out of petrol," Joe explained, "and had to swim back with the *Sleuth*."

Aunt Gertrude sniffed sceptically. "Humph! It must have been some long ride to use up all that fuel!" She hustled off to make hot chocolate.

Mrs Hardy told the boys that their father had left the house an hour before and would be away overnight working on his case. Again Frank and Joe wondered about it. And did the attack tonight have any connection with either case?

After a hot bath and a good night's sleep, Frank and Joe were eager to continue their search for clues to the bowman, the counterfeiters, and the writer of the first warning note to Mr Hardy.

Breakfast over, Frank and Joe went to the lab and dusted the archer's finger guard. To the brothers' delight they lifted one clear print.

"We'll take this to Chief Collig on our way to the paper company in Bridgeport," Frank decided.

Just before they left, Chet telephoned. "Guess what!" he said to Frank, who answered. "I have an appointment at Elekton to see about a job!"

"How'd you do it?" Frank asked, amazed. "You sure work fast."

Chet laughed. "I decided to telephone on my own," he explained. "The man in the personnel office told me there might be something available on a part-time basis. How about that?"

"Swell," Frank said. "The vacancy must have come up since yesterday."

"Funny thing," Chet added. "The personnel manager asked me if I had applied before. I said No, though the guard had phoned about me yesterday. The manager said he didn't remember this, but that somebody else in the office might have taken the call."

Chet became more and more excited as he talked about the prospect of getting a job in the Elekton laboratory. "I'm going to make a lot of money and—"

"Don't get your hopes up too high," Frank cautioned his friend. "Elekton is such a top-secret outfit they might not hire anyone on a part-time basis for lab work. But you might get something else."

"We'll see," Chet replied optimistically.

"Joe and I have something special to show you," Frank told him. "After you have your interview, meet us at the north end of the Bayport waterfront."

Chet begged to know why, but Frank kept the news about the *Sleuth* a secret. "You'll see soon enough," he said.

"Okay, then. So long!"

The Hardys hopped on their motorcycles and rode to police headquarters. They talked to Chief Collig in detail about the attack on them, and left the bowman's fingerprint for him to trace.

"Good work, boys," he said. "I'll let you know what I find out."

Frank and Joe had decided not to mention to him the green truck and its possible connection with the counterfeiters until they had more proof.

The boys mounted their motorcycles and rode to Bridgeport. They easily located the Quality Paper Company, and inquired there for Mr Evans, the sales manager, with whom they had talked the day before.

When Frank and Joe entered his office and identified themselves, Mr Evans looked at the brothers curiously. But he was most co-operative in answering their questions.

"No," Mr Evans said, "we don't sell our star water-mark paper to retail stores in this vicinity. All our purchasers are large industrial companies. Here is a list." He handed a printed sheet across the desk to Frank.

The boys were disappointed not to have obtained any individual's name. Nevertheless, Frank and Joe read the list carefully. Several names, including Elekton Controls Limited, were familiar to them. The warning note could have come from any one of thousands of employees of any of the firms.

"I guess there's no clue here to the man we want to locate," Frank said to Mr Evans.

The boys thanked him. As they started to leave, he called them back.

"Are you boys, by any chance, related to Mr Fenton Hardy?" he asked.

Joe, puzzled, nodded. "He's our father. Why?"

"Quite a coincidence," Mr Evans said. "Mr Hardy was here a little while ago."

"He was!" Frank exclaimed in surprise. The brothers exchanged glances, wondering what mission their father had been on.

"Maybe I shouldn't have mentioned Mr Hardy's visit," Mr Evans said.

"That's all right," Joe assured him. "If Dad had wanted the visit kept secret, he would have told you."

When the boys were outside again, Frank said, "I

hope Dad will be home. I'd like to find out what brought him here."

Frank and Joe rode directly home and were glad to see Mr Hardy's car in the driveway. The boys rushed into the house.

They found the detective in his study, talking on the telephone. The boys paused next to the partly open door.

". . . the same eight-and-one pattern, I believe," their father was saying . . . "Yes—I'll be there . . . Goodbye."

Frank knocked and the boys entered the room. Mr Hardy greeted them warmly. He was startled when Joe told him, "We know where you've been this morning, Dad."

"Were you two shadowing me?" the detective joked.

"Not exactly." Frank grinned, and explained why they had visited the Quality Paper Company.

"Good idea," said the detective. "Did you learn anything?"

"No," Joe replied glumly, then asked suddenly, "Dad, did you go to Quality Paper in connection with he warning note on the arrow?"

Mr Hardy admitted that he had gone there to investigate the watermark. "I believe I did find a clue to confirm a suspicion of mine. But I'm not sure yet where it will lead."

The boys sensed that their father's trip had been linked to his secret case. "If it was to help us on the counterfeiting mystery, he would say so," Frank thought. "And he hasn't mentioned Elekton, so I guess he doesn't suspect any of that company's employees."

Mr Hardy changed the subject. He looked at his sons quizzically. "What's this I hear from Aunt Gertrude about you boys coming home last night half dead?"

The boys explained, omitting none of the details. "We didn't want to alarm Mother and Aunt Gertrude," Frank said, "so we didn't tell them about the attack."

Mr Hardy looked grim and warned his sons gravely to be extra cautious.

"There's one bright spot," he added. "The print you found on that finger guard. It could be a big break."

During lunch the detective was unusually preoccupied. The boys tried to draw him out by questions and deductions about the counterfeiting case. He would say very little, however, and seemed to be concentrating on a knotty problem.

A little later the boys rode their motorcycles straight to the boathouse and parked at the street end of the jetty. "Chet ought to show up soon," Joe remarked.

As the brothers walked towards the boathouse, Frank commented on his father's preoccupation during luncheon.

"I have a hunch Dad's assignment is even tougher than usual," he confided. "I wish we could help him on it."

Frank seemed to be only half listening and nodded absently.

"What's the matter with you?" Joe laughed. "I'm talking to myself!"

Suddenly Frank stopped. He grasped his brother's arm firmly.

"Joe!" he said. "We may have found a clue in Bridgeport this morning and didn't realize it!"

10

The Sign of the Arrow

"WHAT clue do you mean, Frank?" Joe demanded eagerly.

"Elekton's name was on that list Mr Evans showed us this morning."

"Yes, I know. But Dad didn't seem excited over that."

"Well, I am," Frank said. "Put two and two together. Every time we've been near the Elekton area, something has happened. First, the warning on the arrow, then the attack last night."

"Of course!" Joe said. "I get you! Someone who has access to the company's paper supply could have sent the warnings, and knocked us out. But who? An employee of Elekton?"

"That's the mystery," said Frank. "Is the person trying to get at Dad through us? And which of the cases is this mysterious person connected with—the counterfeit case, or Dad's secret one?"

"Then there's the bike," Joe recalled. "Someone from the company could easily have taken it from the storage area under the mill at night when the guard and maintenance man were inside the gatehouse."

"Joe," said Frank slowly, "we're theorizing on the

case having a connection with Elekton. Do you think Dad is too, even though he didn't tell us? The Elekton name may have been the clue *he* found at Quality Paper!"

Joe snapped his fingers. "My guess is that Dad is doing some detective work for Elekton! That would explain why he can't say anything. Elekton *is* doing top-secret space missile work."

"It's possible," Frank speculated, "that Elekton retained Dad because of the chain of sabotage acts in plants handling similar jobs for the government."

"Sounds logical," Joe agreed. "I guess Dad's main assignment would be to ward off sabotage at Elekton. No wonder he is so anxious to find out who sent the warnings."

Just then Chet arrived in the Queen and leaped out. "I have a job!" he announced to Frank and Joe. Then he looked a bit sheepish. "It's—er—in the cafeteria, serving behind the food counter. The cafeteria is run on a concession basis, and the people working there aren't as carefully screened as the plant employees."

Joe grinned. "It's not very scientific, but think of the food! You'll be able to eat anything you want."

Chet sighed, and did not respond with one of his usual humorous comebacks. A worried expression spread over his face. He shifted from one foot to the other.

"What's on your mind?" Joe prodded. "Not nervous about the job, are you?"

Chet shook his head. He dug into his pocket and pulled out a piece of white paper. "I *am* nervous about this—another warning note! It was on the seat of my car when I came out after the job interview." He handed the note to Frank.

Unfolding it, Frank read aloud, " '*You and your pals watch out!*' " There was no signature on the boldly printed note, but at the bottom was the crude drawing of an arrow.

Chet gulped. "Must be that arrow shooter. He's keeping tabs on all of us!" he said.

Frank and Joe studied the note intently for a minute, then Frank asked Chet, "Where did you park?"

"Near the front entrance. The guard at the mill told me to go in that way to reach the personnel office." Chet smiled faintly. "Boy, was *he* surprised when I told him I had an appointment."

The Hardys were more convinced than ever that their unknown enemy must somehow be linked with the Elekton company. "We'll compare this note with the others," Frank said. "But first, Chet, we'll show you something to cheer you up."

The brothers led their friend into the boathouse. "Feast your eyes!" Joe grinned. "This is our surprise."

Chet gasped when he saw the *Sleuth*. "Wow! She's really yours?"

"You bet! How about a ride?"

Eagerly Chet accepted. As the Hardys refuelled from the boathouse tank, they told Chet about the adventure they had had the previous night.

"You suspect there's a connection between somebody at Elekton and the counterfeiting?" Chet guessed.

"That's right," Frank replied.

He then told Chet about the Pritos having received a

counterfeit bill. "We think," said Joe, "the boy in the panel truck who gave Mike the counterfeit twenty *might* have been Ken Blake."

"Ken Blake again," Chet commented. "Funny how he keeps turning up."

The Hardys agreed. As Frank steered the *Sleuth* into the bay, Joe suggested, "Let's run up Willow River to the mill. That'll give you a good chance to see how the boat rides, Chet, and also we can stop to question the guard and maintenance man, and Ken Blake. They might have seen some suspicious people in the area."

"I should've known this would turn into a sleuthing trip." Chet sighed. "Oh, well, I'm with you if we can learn anything about the counterfeiters."

When Frank had the *Sleuth* well away from shore and out of the path of other craft on the bay, he pushed the throttle for more speed and steered the boat towards the mouth of the river.

The *Sleuth* responded like a thoroughbred. The stern sat back in the water and in a second it was planing wide open across the bay.

"How do you like this?" Frank called from the cockpit.

"Terrific!" Chet yelled back enthusiastically.

Frank now swung the wheel back and forth to show his friend how stable the boat was. Then he said, "Joe, take the wheel and show Chet your stuff!"

The brothers changed places and Joe made a wide circle to port, with the *Sleuth* heeling beautifully. Then he headed for the river's narrow mouth.

"Better slow down!" Frank warned him.

Obediently Joe began to ease the throttle. The

Sleuth did not respond! And there was no lessening of the roar of the engine.

Quickly Joe turned the throttle all the way back. Still there was no decrease in speed.

"Something's wrong!" he shouted. "I can't slow her down!"

11

Sinister Tactics

"WHAT do you mean you can't slow down?" Chet yelled. "Turn off the engine!"

"Joe can't," Frank said grimly. "He has the throttle to *off* position and we're still travelling at full speed."

There was no choice for Joe but to swing the *Sleuth* into another wide, sweeping turn. It would have been foolhardy to enter the river at such speed, and Joe knew that under the circumstances he needed lots of room to manœuvre. The motorboat zoomed back into the middle of the bay. It seemed to the boys that suddenly there was far more traffic on the bay than there had been before.

"Look out!" Chet yelled. Joe just missed a high-speed runabout.

He turned and twisted to avoid the small pleasure boats. The young pilot was more worried about endangering these people than he was about colliding with the larger vessels, which were commercial craft.

"Keep her as straight as you can!" Frank shouted to Joe. "I'll take a look at the engine and see what I can do with it."

Frank stood up and leaned forward to open the cowling in front of the dashboard, as the boat leaped across the waves in the bay.

"Watch out!" Chet yelled, as Frank almost lost his balance.

Joe made a sharp turn to avoid cutting in front of a rowboat containing a man and several children. Joe realized that the wash of the speeding *Sleuth* might upset it.

"If those people are thrown overboard," he thought, "we'll have to rescue them. But how?" Fortunately, the boat did not overturn.

Frank quickly lifted the cowling from the engine and stepped into the pit. He knew he could open the fuel intake and siphon off the petrol into the bay, but this would take too long.

"I'll have to stop the boat—right now!" he decided.

Frank reached down beside the roaring engine and pulled three wires away from the distributor. Instantly the engine died, and Frank stood up just as Joe made another sharp turn to miss hitting a small outboard motorboat that had wandered across their path.

"Good grief!" Chet cried out. "That was a close one!"

Even with the *Sleuth*'s reduction in speed, the other boat rocked violently back and forth as it was caught in the wash. Frank grasped the gunwale, ready to leap over the side and rescue the man if his boat overturned.

But the smaller craft had been pulled round to face the wash. Though it bounced almost out of the water, the boat quickly resumed an even keel.

The lone man in it kept coming towards the *Sleuth*. As he drew alongside, he began to wave his arms and shout at the boys.

"What's the matter with you young fools?" he

yelled. "You shouldn't be allowed to operate a boat until you learn how to run one."

"We couldn't—" Joe started to say when the man interrupted.

"You should have more respect for other people's safety!"

Frank finally managed to explain. "It was an accident. The throttle was jammed open. I had to pull the wires out of the distributor to stop her."

By this time the outboard was close enough for its pilot to look over the *Sleuth*'s side and into the engine housing where Frank was pointing at the distributor.

The man quickly calmed down. "Sorry, boys," he said. "There are so many fools running around in high-powered boats these days, without knowing anything about the rules of navigation, I just got good and mad at your performance."

"I don't blame you, sir," said Joe. Then he asked, "Do you think you could tow us into the municipal dock so that we can have repairs made?"

"Glad to," said the man.

At the dock, the Hardys and Chet watched while the serviceman checked the *Sleuth* to find out the cause of the trouble. Presently he looked up at the boys with an odd expression.

"What's the trouble?" Frank asked. "Serious?"

The mechanic's reply startled them. "This is a new motorboat and no doubt was in tiptop shape. But somebody tampered with the throttle!"

"What!" Joe demanded. "Let's see!"

The serviceman pointed out where a cotter pin had been removed from the throttle group. And the tension spring which opened and closed the valve had been replaced with a bar to hold the throttle wide open, once it was pushed there.

The Hardys and Chet exchanged glances which meant: "The unknown enemy again?"

The boys, however, did not mention their suspicions to the mechanic. Frank merely requested him to make the necessary repairs on the *Sleuth*. Then the trio walked back to the Hardys' boathouse.

Several fishermen were standing at a nearby wharf. Frank and Joe asked them if they had seen anyone near the boathouse.

"No," each one said.

The three boys inspected the boathouse. Frank scrutinized the hasp on the door. "The *Sleuth* must have been tampered with while it was inside. Unless it was done last night while we were unconscious."

There was no sign of the lock having been forced open, but near the edge of the loose hasp there were faint scratches.

"Look!" Joe pointed. "Somebody tore the whole hasp off the door and then carefully put it back on."

Frank looked grim. "I'm sure this was done by the same person who attacked us last night, and sent us the warnings."

"You're right," said Joe. "This is what Dad would call sinister tactics."

Again both brothers wondered with which case their enemy was concerned. There seemed to be no answer to this tantalizing question which kept coming up again and again.

Chet drove the Queen back to the Hardys', and the

brothers rode their motorcycles. When they reached the house they went at once to the lab with the note Chet had found in his car.

They dusted it for fingerprints but were disappointed again. There was not one trace of a print. The boys found, however, that the paper was the same as that used for the previous warnings.

"Well," said Joe, "I vote we go on out to the mill."

The boys went in the Queen. Chet had just brought his car to a stop on the dirt road when Joe called out, "There's Ken Blake trimming the grass over by the mill-race. Now's our chance to talk to him."

The three jumped out. Ken looked up, stared for a second, then threw his clippers to the ground. To the boys' surprise, he turned and ran away from them, along the stream.

"Wait!" Frank yelled.

Ken looked over his shoulder, but kept on running. Suddenly he tripped and stumbled. For a moment the boy swayed on the bank of the rushing stream. The next instant he lost his balance and fell headlong into the water!

At once the Hardys and Chet dashed to the water's edge. Horrified, they saw that the force of the water was carrying the boy, obviously a poor swimmer, straight towards the plunging falls!

12

An Interrupted Chase

FRANK, quick as lightning, dashed to the mill-stream and plunged in after Ken Blake. The boy was being pulled relentlessly towards the waterfall. In another moment he would be swept over the brink of the dam!

With strong strokes, Frank swam towards the struggling boy. Reaching out desperately, he managed to grasp Ken's shirt.

Joe jumped in to assist Frank. The two boys were buffeted by the rushing water, but between them they managed to drag Ken back from the falls.

"Easy," Frank cautioned the frightened youth. "Relax. We'll have you out in a jiffy."

Despite the weight of their clothes, the Hardys, both proficient at lifesaving techniques, soon worked Ken close to the bank. Chet leaned over and helped haul him out of the water. Then Frank and Joe climbed out.

To their relief, Ken, though white-faced and panting from exhaustion, seemed to be all right. The Hardys flopped to the ground to catch their breath.

"That was a whale of a rescue!" Chet praised them.

"You bet!" Ken gasped weakly. "Thanks, fellows! You've saved my life!"

"In a way it was our fault," Joe replied ruefully.

"You wouldn't have fallen in if we hadn't come here. But why *did* you run away when you saw us?"

Ken hesitated before answering. "Mr Markel—the guard at the gatehouse—said you wanted to talk to me. He warned me about talking to outsiders, because of the strict security at Elekton."

Joe nodded. "We understand, Ken. But," he added, "we have something important to ask you, and I don't think you will be going against company rules if you answer. Did anybody use your bike the night before last to deliver a message to our house?"

"Your house?" Ken sounded surprised. "No. At least, not that I know of."

Joe went on, "Did you buy a pedal in Bridgeport to replace the one missing from your bike?"

Ken again looked surprised. "Yes. It was gone yesterday morning when I came to work. I suspected someone must have used my bike and lost the pedal. When I couldn't find it around here, Mr Markel sent me to Bridgeport to buy a new one."

It was on the tip of Frank's tongue to ask the boy if he had seen any person in the area of the mill carrying a bow and arrow. But suddenly Mr Markel and the maintenance man came dashing from the mill.

"What's going on here?" the guard demanded, staring at the Hardys and Ken, who were still dripping wet.

Briefly, Frank told the men what had happened. They thanked the brothers warmly for the rescue, and the maintenance man hustled Ken into the mill for dry clothes. He did not invite the Hardys inside.

Frank and Joe turned to Mr Markel, intending to

question him. But before they could, a horn sounded and a shabby, green panel truck approached the plant gate.

The guard hurried over to admit the truck and it entered without stopping. Suddenly Joe grabbed Frank's arm. "Hey! That truck's unmarked—it looks like the one Tony described."

The brothers peered after the vehicle, but by this time it was far into the grounds and had turned out of sight behind one of the buildings.

"I wonder," Joe said excitedly, "if the driver is the man who gave the Pritos the counterfeit bill!"

The boys had noticed only that the driver wore a cap pulled low and sat slouched over the wheel.

"If this truck's the same one, it may be connected with Elekton," Frank said tersely.

Both Hardys, though uncomfortably wet, decided to stay and see what they could find out. They hailed Mr Markel as he walked back from the Elekton gate.

"Does that truck belong to Elekton?" Frank asked him.

"No, it doesn't," the guard answered.

"Do you know who does own it?" asked Joe.

Mr Markel shook his head regretfully. "Sorry, boys. I'm afraid I'm not allowed to give out such information. Excuse me, I have work to do." He turned and went back into the gatehouse.

"Come on, fellows," Chet urged. "You'd better not hang around in those wet clothes."

The Hardys, however, were determined to stay long enough to question Ken Blake further, if possible.

"He'll probably be coming outside soon," said Joe.

"Frank and I can dry out on the beach by the cave. It won't take long in this hot sun."

Chet sighed. "Okay. And I know what I'm supposed to do—wait here and watch for Ken."

Frank chuckled. "You're a mind reader."

Chet took his post at the edge of the woods, and the Hardys hurried down to the river's edge.

They spread their slacks and shirts on the sun-warmed rocks. In a short while the clothing was dry enough to put on.

"Say, maybe we'll have time to investigate that tunnel before Chet calls us," Joe suggested eagerly.

He and Frank started for the cave, but a second later Chet came running through the woods towards them.

"Ken came out, but he's gone on an errand," he reported, and explained that the boy had rushed from the mill dressed in oversize dungarees and a red shirt. "He was riding off on his bike when I caught up to him. I told Ken you wanted to see him, but he said he had to make a fast trip downtown and deliver an envelope to the Parker Building."

"We'll catch him there," Frank decided.

The three boys ran up the wooded slope and jumped into the Queen. They kept on the main road to Bayport, hoping to overtake Ken, but they did not pass him.

"He must have taken another route," Joe said.

At the Parker Building there were no parking spaces available, so Chet stopped his jalopy long enough to drop off Frank and Joe.

"I'll keep circling the block until you come out," Chet called as he drove away.

There was no sign of Ken's bicycle outside the building. The Hardys rushed into the lobby and immediately were met by a five o'clock crowd of office workers streaming from the elevators. Frank and Joe made their way through the throng, but saw no sign of Ken.

Joe had an idea. "Maybe he was making the delivery to Mr Peters, the name I saw on the Manila envelope I picked up the other day. Let's see if Ken's still in his office."

The boys ran their eyes down the building directory, but Mr Peters was not listed. The brothers questioned the elevator starter, who replied that so far as he knew, no one by the name of Peters had an office in the building.

Joe asked the starter, "Did you notice a boy wearing dungarees and a bright red shirt in the lobby a few minutes ago?"

"Sure," was the prompt reply. "Just before the five o'clock rush started. I saw the boy come in and give an envelope to a man waiting in the corner over there. The man took the envelope and they both left right away."

"I guess he must be Mr Peters," Frank said.

"Could be," the starter agreed. "I didn't recognize him."

As the Hardys hurried outside, Joe said, "Well, we got crossed up on that one. Let's get back to the mill. Ken will have to drop off the bike."

The brothers waited at the kerb for Chet. In a few minutes the Queen pulled up. "All aboard!" Chet sang out. "Any luck?"

"No."

When Frank told Chet they were returning to the

mill, their good-natured friend nodded. "It's fortunate I bought these sandwiches," he said, indicating a paper bag on the seat beside him. "I had a feeling we'd be late for supper."

Joe snapped his fingers. "That reminds me. I'll stop and phone our families so they won't hold back supper for us."

After Joe had made the calls and they were on their way again, he told Frank and Chet that Mr Hardy had left a message saying he would not be home until after ten o'clock.

As the Queen went down the side road past the Elekton buildings, Frank thought, "If Dad *is* working for Elekton, he might be somewhere in the plant right this minute."

The same possibility was running through Joe's mind. "Wonder if Dad is expecting a break in his secret case."

As Chet neared the turn into the mill road, a green truck zoomed out directly in front of the Queen. Chet jammed on his brake, narrowly avoiding a collision. The truck swung round the jalopy at full speed and roared off towards the highway.

"The green truck we saw before!" Joe exclaimed. "This time I got the licence number, but couldn't see the driver's face."

"Let's follow him!" Frank urged.

Chet started back in pursuit. "That guy ought to be arrested for reckless driving!" he declared indignantly.

The Hardys peered ahead as they turned right on to the main road, trying to keep the truck in sight.

Suddenly the boys heard a tremendous *bo-o-om* and felt the car shake.

"An explosion!" Joe cried out, turning his head. "Look!"

Against the sky a brilliant flash and billows of smoke came from the direction of Elekton. Another explosion followed.

"The plant's blowing up!" Joe gasped.

· 13 ·

Sudden Suspicion

THE roar of the explosion and the sight of smoke and flames stunned the three boys for a moment. Chet stepped on the brake so fast that his passengers hit the dashboard.

"Take it easy!" urged Frank, although he was as excited as Chet.

All thoughts of chasing the mysterious green truck were erased from the Hardys' minds.

"Let's get as close as possible," Frank said tersely, as Chet headed the car back towards the plant. "I'd like to know what—"

Frank broke off as a series of explosions occurred. The brothers sat forward tensely.

As the Queen drew near the main entrance, the boys could see that the flames and smoke were pouring from a single building at the north-east corner.

"It's one of the labs, I think," said Frank.

Quickly Chet pulled over and parked, and the boys hopped out of the jalopy. The series of explosive sounds had died away, but the damage appeared to be extensive. Most of the windows in the steel-and-concrete building had been blown out by the force of the blast.

Smoke and flames were pouring out of the blackened

spaces where the windows had been. As the boys ran towards the front, the roof of the west wing caved in. The rush of oxygen provided fuel for a new surge of flames that reached towards the sky.

"Lucky this happened after closing time," Chet murmured, staring wide-eyed at the fire. "There might have been a lot of injuries."

"I hope no one was inside." Joe exchanged worried glances with his brother. Both shared the same concern. It was for their father.

"I wish we could find out whether or not Dad's at Elekton," Frank whispered to Joe.

At this point the boys heard the scream of sirens. Soon fire trucks and police cars from Bayport pulled up at the front gate. The Hardys saw Chief Collig in the first police car. They rushed up to him and he asked how they happened to be there.

"Sleuthing," Frank answered simply. Without going into detail, he added, "Joe and I aren't sure, but we have a hunch Dad may have been—or still is—here at Elekton. All right if we go into the grounds and look round?" he asked eagerly. "And take Chet?"

The officer agreed.

By this time the guard had opened the wide gate, and the fire apparatus rushed in. Some of the police officers followed, while others took positions along the road and directed traffic so that it would not block the path of emergency vehicles.

As the boys rode inside with the chief, Joe asked him, "Any idea what caused the explosion?"

"Not yet. Hard to tell until the firemen can get inside the building."

When they reached the burning structure, Chief Collig began directing police operations, and checking with the firemen. As soon as they seemed to have the flames under control, the firemen entered the laboratory building to look for any possible victims of the explosions.

The Hardys and Chet, meanwhile, had searched the outside area for Mr Hardy, but did not see the detective.

"Maybe we were wrong about Dad's coming here," Joe said to his brother, more hopeful than before. "Dad probably wouldn't have been in the lab."

The brothers went back to Chief Collig, who told them he had not seen Fenton Hardy. Just then the fire chief came up to the group.

"I'll bet this fire was no accident," he reported grimly to Collig. "The same thing happened in Indiana about two months ago—and that was sabotage!"

Frank and Joe stared at each other. "Sabotage!" Joe whispered.

A startling thought flashed into Frank's mind and, drawing his brother aside, he exclaimed, "Remember what we overheard Dad say on the phone? 'The same eight-and-one pattern. I'll be there.' "

"And two months equal about eight weeks," Joe added excitedly. "That might have been the saboteurs' time schedule Dad was referring to! So maybe the explosion at Elekton was set for today!"

Frank's apprehension about his father returned full force. "Joe," he said tensely, "Dad might have been inside the lab building trying to stop the saboteurs!"

Deeply disturbed, the Hardys pleaded with Chief

Collig for permission to enter the building and search for their father.

"I can tell you're worried, boys," the officer said sympathetically. "But it's still too risky for me to let you go inside. It'll be some time before we're sure there's no danger of further explosions."

"I know," Frank agreed. "But what if Dad *is* in there and badly hurt?"

The police chief did his best to reassure the brothers. "Your father would never forgive me if I let you risk your lives," he added. "I suggest that you go on home and cheer up your mother in case she has the same fears you do. I promise if I see your dad I'll call you, or ask him to."

The boys realized that their old friend was right, and slowly walked away. Frank and Joe looked back once at the blackened building, outlined against the twilight sky. Wisps of smoke still curled from the torn-out windows. It was a gloomy, silent trio that drove to the Hardy home in the Queen.

Frank and Joe decided not to tell their mother or aunt of their fear, or to give any hint of their suspicions. When the boys entered the living-room, both women gave sighs of relief. They had heard the explosions and the subsequent news flashes about it.

Aunt Gertrude looked at the boys sharply. "By the way, where have you three been all this time? I was afraid that you might have been near Elekton's."

Frank, Joe and Chet admitted that they had been. "You know we couldn't miss a chance to find out what the excitement was about," Joe said teasingly, then added with an assurance he was far from feeling,

"Don't worry. The fire was pretty much under control when we left."

To change the subject, Frank said cheerfully, "I sure am hungry. Let's dig into those sandwiches you bought, Chet!"

"Good idea!" Joe agreed.

"Are you sure you don't want me to make you something hot to eat?" Mrs Hardy asked.

"Thanks, Mother, but we'll have enough." Frank smiled.

Chet called his family to let them know where he was, then the three boys sat down in the kitchen and halfheartedly munched the sandwiches. Aunt Gertrude bustled in and served them generous portions of deep-dish apple pie.

"This is even more super than usual," Chet said, trying hard to be cheerful.

The boys finished their pie, but without appetite. When they refused second helpings, however, Aunt Gertrude demanded suspiciously, "Are you ill—or what?"

"Oh, no, Aunty," Joe replied hastily. "Just—er—too much detecting."

"I can believe that!" Miss Hardy said tartly.

The evening dragged on, tension mounting every minute. The boys tried to read or talk, but their concern for the detective's safety made it impossible to concentrate on anything else.

Eleven o'clock! Where *was* their father? Frank and Joe wondered.

"Aren't you boys going to bed soon?" Mrs Hardy asked, as she and Aunt Gertrude started upstairs.

"Pretty soon," Frank answered.

The three boys sat glumly in the living-room for a few minutes until the women were out of earshot.

"Fellows," said Chet, "I caught on that you're sure your dad is working on an important case for Elekton, and it's a top-secret one—that's why you couldn't say anything about it."

"You're right," Frank told him.

Chet went on to mention that his father had heard of various problems at Elekton—production stoppages caused by power breaks, and, before the buildings were completed, reports of tools and equipment going missing.

"This ties in with our hunch about the secrecy of Dad's case," Frank said. "The company must have suspected that major sabotage was being planned, and retained Dad to try and stop it."

Talking over their speculations helped to relieve some of the tension the boys felt and made the time pass a little faster as they waited for news of Fenton Hardy.

"I wonder how the saboteurs got into the plant?" Joe said, thinking aloud. "Both the gates are locked and well guarded. It seems almost impossible for anyone to have sneaked in the necessary amount of explosives—without inside help."

A sudden thought flashed into Frank's mind. He leaped to his feet. "The green truck!" he exclaimed. "It was unmarked, remember? It could have been carrying dynamite—camouflaged under ordinary supplies!"

"That could be, Frank!" Joe jumped up. "If so, no

wonder it was in such a rush! I'll phone the chief right now and give him the truck's licence number."

Frank went with Joe to the hall telephone. As they approached the phone, it rang. The bell, shattering the tense atmosphere, seemed louder than usual.

"It must be Dad!" exclaimed the brothers together, and Chet hurried into the hall.

Frank eagerly lifted the receiver. "Hello!" he said expectantly.

The next moment Frank looked dejected. He replaced the receiver and said glumly, "Wrong number."

The Hardys exchanged bleak looks. What *had* happened to their father?

14

Prisoners!

THE Hardys' disappointment in discovering that the telephone call was not from their father was intense. Nevertheless, Joe picked up the receiver and dialled police headquarters to report the truck's licence number.

"Line's busy," he said.

Joe tried several more times without success. Suddenly he burst out, "I can't stand it another minute to think of Dad perhaps lying out there hurt. Let's go back to Elekton and see if we can learn something."

"All right," Frank agreed, also eager for action, and the three rushed to the front door.

Just as they opened it, the boys saw the headlights of a car turning into the driveway.

"*It's Dad!*" Joe barely refrained from shouting so as not to awaken Mrs Hardy and Aunt Gertrude.

The detective's saloon headed for the garage at the back of the house. Heaving sighs of thankful relief, the boys quietly hurried through the house into the kitchen to meet him.

"Are we glad to see you, Dad!" Frank exclaimed as he came into the house.

His father looked pale and dishevelled. There was a

large purple bruise on his left temple. He slumped wearily into a chair.

"I guess I'm lucky to be here." Mr Hardy managed a rueful smile. "Well, I owe you boys an explanation, and now is the time."

"Dad," Joe spoke up, "you *are* working on the sabotage case for Elekton, aren't you?"

"And you were in the lab building during the explosions?" Frank put in.

"You're both right," the detective replied. "Of course I know I can depend on all of you to keep the matter strictly confidential. The case is far from solved."

Mr Hardy was relieved that Frank and Joe had kept their fears for his safety from his wife and sister. He now revealed to the boys that for the past several hours he had been closeted with Elekton's officials. Suspecting that the saboteurs had inside help, the detective had screened the records of all employees. He and the officials had found nothing suspicious.

"I'll submit a full report to the FBI tomorrow morning, and continue a search on my own."

When Joe asked if the eight-and-one pattern referred to the saboteurs' schedule, his father nodded. "In the other plants, the sabotage took place eight weeks plus one day apart.

"In each of those plants," the detective went on, "the damage occurred right after closing time. Figuring the schedule would be exactly right for an attempt on Elekton in a couple of days, I started a systematic check of the various buildings. I planned to check daily, until the saboteurs had been caught here or elsewhere. At my request, one company security guard was assigned to assist me. I felt that the fewer people who knew what I was doing, the better. That's how I ruined the saboteurs' plan in Detroit.

"Nothing suspicious occurred here until today when I took up a post in the section of the building where the experimental work is being conducted. After all the employees had left, and the dim night-lights were on, I went towards the east lab wing to investigate."

Mr Hardy paused, took a deep breath, and continued, "Just as I reached the lab, I happened to glance back into the hall. Things started to happen—fast."

"What did you see, Dad?" asked Joe, and all the boys leaned forward expectantly.

The detective went on, "Hurrying down the hall from the west lab were two men in work clothes, one carrying a leather bag. I knew there weren't supposed to be any workmen in the building. I stepped out to question them, but the pair broke into a run and dashed past me down the stairs."

"Did you see what either of them looked like?" Frank asked.

"I did catch a glimpse of one before they broke away. He had heavy features and thick eyebrows. But just as I was about to take off after them, I smelled something burning in the east lab and went to investigate. The first thing I saw was a long fuse sputtering towards a box of dynamite, set against the wall.

"I didn't know if it was the kind of fuse that would burn internally or not, so I took my penknife and cut it close to the dynamite. Professional saboteurs don't usually rely on just one explosive, so I started for the west wing to check the lab there."

Mr Hardy leaned back in his chair and rubbed the bruise on his temple. In a low voice he said, "But I didn't make it. I was running towards the hall when there was a roar and a burst of flame. The explosion lifted me off my feet and threw me against the wall. Though I was stunned, I managed to get back to the east wing. I reached for the phone, then blacked out.

"I must have been unconscious for some time, because when the firemen found me and helped me out of the building, the fire had been put out."

"You're all right now?" asked Frank.

"Yes. It was a temporary blackout from shock. What bothers me is that I had the saboteurs' pattern figured out—only they must have become panicky and moved forward their nefarious scheme by two days."

Joe looked grim. "I wish we'd been there to help you capture those rats!"

Chet asked Mr Hardy if he would like a fruit drink. "I'll make some lemonade," he offered.

"Sounds good." Mr Hardy smiled.

As they sipped the lemonade, Frank and Joe questioned their father about his theories.

"I'm still convinced," said Mr Hardy, "that one of those men works in the plant. How else would he have known when the watchman makes his rounds and how to disconnect the electronic alarms? But I *can't* figure how the outside accomplice got in—those gates are carefully guarded."

At this point Frank told his father about the green truck. "We suspected at first it might be connected with the counterfeiters. Now we have a hunch the saboteurs may have used it."

Fenton Hardy seemed greatly encouraged by this possible lead. Joe gave him the licence number, which Mr Hardy said he would report to Chief Collig at once.

When Mr Hardy returned from the telephone, he told the boys the chief would check the licence number with the Motor Vehicle Bureau in the morning and by then he would also have some information about the print on the archer's finger guard.

The next morning after breakfast Frank said he wanted to take another look at the warning notes.

"Why?" Joe asked curiously, as they went to the file.

Frank held up the "arrow" warning, and the one received by Chet. "I've been thinking about the printing on these two—seems familiar. I have it!" he burst out.

"Have what?" Joe asked.

"This printing"—Frank pointed to the papers—"is the same as the printing on Ken's envelope addressed to Victor Peters. I'm positive."

Excitedly the brothers speculated on the possible meaning of this clue. "I'd sure like to find out," said Joe, "who addresses the envelopes Ken delivers, and if they're always sent to Mr Peters in the Parker Building. And why—if he doesn't have an office there. And who *is* Victor Peters?"

"If the person who addresses the envelopes and the sender of the warnings are the same," Frank declared, "it looks as though he's sending something to a confederate, under pretence of having work done for Elekton. I wonder what that something could be?"

"At any rate," Joe added, "this could be a link

either to the counterfeiters or to the saboteurs. Which one?"

The boys decided to go out to the mill again, in the hope of quizzing Ken Blake. Just then their father came downstairs. Frank and Joe were glad to see that he looked rested and cheerful.

Mr Hardy phoned Chief Collig. When the detective hung up, he told his sons that the licence number belonged to stolen plates and the fingerprint to a confidence man nicknamed The Arrow.

"He's called this because for several years he worked at exclusive summer resorts, teaching archery to wealthy vacationers, then fleecing as many of them as he could. After each swindle, The Arrow disappeared. Unfortunately, there's no picture of him on file. All the police have is a general description of him."

Frank and Joe learned that the swindler had a pleasant speaking voice, was of medium height, with dark hair and brown eyes.

"Not much to go on," Joe remarked glumly.

"No, but if he *is* working for Elekton, he must be pretty shrewd to have passed their screening."

Mr Hardy agreed, and phoned Elekton, requesting the personnel department to check if anybody answering The Arrow's description was employed there.

The brothers then informed their father about the similar lettering on the warnings and Ken's Manila envelope.

"A valuable clue," he remarked. "I wish I could go with you to question Ken." The detective explained that right now he had to make his report of the explosion to the nearby FBI office.

When he had left, Frank and Joe rode off to the mill on their motorcycles.

At the gatehouse the guard had unexpected news. "Ken Blake isn't working here any more," Mr Markel said. "We had to discharge him."

"Why?" asked Joe in surprise.

The guard replied that most of the necessary jobs had been done around the mill grounds. "Mr Docker—my co-worker—and I felt we could handle everything from now on," he explained.

"I see," said Frank. "Can you tell us where Ken is staying?"

Markel said he was not sure, but he thought Ken might have been boarding in an old farmhouse about a mile up the highway.

When the brothers reached the highway, they stopped. "Which way do we go? Mr Markel didn't tell us," Joe said in chagrin.

"Instead of going back to find out, let's ask at that petrol station across the way," Frank suggested. "Someone there may know."

"An old farmhouse?" the attendant repeated in answer to Frank's query. "There's one about a mile from here going towards Bayport. That might be the place your friend is staying. What does he look like?"

Frank described Ken carefully. The attendant nodded. "Yep. I've seen him ride by here on his bike. A couple of times when I was going past the farm I noticed him turn in at the farm road."

"Thanks a lot!" The Hardys cycled off quickly.

Soon they were heading up the narrow, dusty lane, which led to a ramshackle, weather-beaten house. The brothers parked their motorcycles among the high weeds in front of it and dismounted.

"This place seems deserted!" Joe muttered.

Frank agreed and looked around, perplexed. "Odd that Ken would be boarding in such a run-down house."

Frank and Joe walked on to the creaky porch and knocked at the sagging door. There was no answer. They knocked again and called. Still no response.

"Some peculiar boarding-house!" Joe said. "I wouldn't want a room here!"

Frank frowned. "This must be the wrong place. Look—it's all locked up and there's hardly any furniture."

"I'll bet nobody lives in this house!" Joe burst out.

"But the attendant said he has seen Ken riding in here," Frank declared. "Why?"

"Let's have a look," Joe urged.

Mystified, Frank and Joe circled the house. Since they were now certain it had been abandoned, they glanced in various windows. When Joe came to the kitchen he grabbed Frank's arm excitedly.

"Somebody *is* staying here! Could it be Ken?"

Through the dusty glass the boys could see on a rickety table several open cans of food, a carton of milk, and a bowl.

"Must be a tramp," Frank guessed. "I'm sure Ken wouldn't live here."

In turning away, the young detectives noticed a small stone structure about ten yards behind the house. It was the size of a one-car garage. Instead of windows, it had slits high in the walls.

"It probably was used to store farm equipment," Frank said. "We might as well check."

They unbolted the old-fashioned, stout, wooden double doors. These swung outwards, and the boys were surprised that the doors opened so silently. "As if they'd been oiled," Frank said.

"No wonder!" Joe cried out. "Look!"

Inside was a shabby, green panel truck! "The same one we saw yesterday!" Joe exclaimed. "What's it doing here?"

The boys noticed immediately that the vehicle had no number plates. "They were probably taken off," Frank surmised, "and disposed of."

Frank checked the glove compartment while Joe looked on the seat and under the cushion for any clue to the driver or owner of the vehicle. Suddenly he called out, "Hey! What's going on?"

Joe jumped from the truck and saw with astonishment that the garage doors were swinging shut. Together, the boys rushed forward but not in time. They heard the outside bolt being rammed into place.

"We're prisoners!" Frank exclaimed.

Again and again the Hardys threw their weight against the doors. This proved futile. Panting, Frank and Joe looked for a means of escape.

"Those slits in the wall are too high and too narrow anyway," Frank said, chiding himself for not having been on guard.

Finally he reached into the glove compartment and drew out an empty cigarette package he had noticed before. He pulled off the foil. Joe understood immediately what his brother had in mind. Frank lifted the truck's hood and jammed the foil between the starting wires near the fuse box. "Worth a try," he said. "Ignition key's gone. If we can start the engine—we'll smash our way out!"

Joe took his place at the wheel and Frank climbed in beside him. To their delight, Joe gunned the engine into life.

"Here goes!" he muttered grimly. "Brace yourself!"

"Ready!"

Joe eased the truck as far back as he could, then accelerated swiftly forward. The truck's wheels spun on the dirt floor and then with a roar it headed for the heavy doors.

15

Lead to a Counterfeiter

C-R-A-S-H! The green truck smashed through the heavy garage doors. The Hardys felt a terrific jolt and heard the wood splinter and rip as they shot forward into the farmyard.

"Wow!" Joe gasped, as he braked to a halt. "We're free—but not saying in what shape!"

Frank gave a wry laugh. "Probably better than the front of this truck!"

The boys hopped to the ground and looked around the overgrown yard. No one was in sight. The whole area seemed just as deserted as it had been when they arrived.

"Let's check the house," Joe urged. "Someone *could* be hiding in there."

The brothers ran to the run-down dwelling. They found all the doors and windows locked. Again they peered through the dirty panes, but did not see anyone.

"I figure that whoever locked us in the garage would decide that getting away from here in a hurry was his safest bet."

"He must have gone on foot," Joe remarked. "I didn't hear an engine start up."

The Hardys decided to separate, each searching the highway for a mile in opposite directions.

"We'll meet back at the service station we stopped at," Frank called as the boys kicked their motors into life and took off towards the highway.

Fifteen minutes later they parked near the station. Neither boy had spotted any suspicious pedestrians.

"Did you see anybody come down this road in a hurry during the past twenty minutes?" Joe asked the attendant.

"I didn't notice, fellows," came the answer. "I've been busy working under a car. Find your friend?"

"No. That farmhouse is apparently deserted except for signs of a tramp living there," Joe told him.

The Hardys quickly asked the attendant if he knew of any boarding-house nearby. After a moment's thought, he replied:

"I believe a Mrs Smith, who lives a little way beyond the old place, takes boarders."

"We'll try there. Thanks again," Frank said, as he and Joe went back to their motorcycles.

Before Frank threw his weight back on the starter, he said, "Well, let's hope Ken Blake can give us a lead."

"If we ever find him," Joe responded.

They located Mrs Smith's boarding-house with no trouble. She was a pleasant, middle-aged woman and quickly confirmed that Ken was staying there for the summer. She was an old friend of his parents. Mrs Smith invited the Hardys to sit down in the living-room.

"Ken's upstairs now," she said. "I'll call him."

When Ken came down the Hardys noticed that he looked dejected. Frank felt certain it was because of losing his job and asked him what had happened.

"I don't know," Ken replied. "Mr Markel just told me I wouldn't be needed any longer. I hope I'll be able to find another job this summer," he added. "My folks sent me here for a vacation. But I was going to surprise them—" His voice trailed off sadly.

"Ken," Frank said kindly, "you may be able to help us in a very important way. Now that you're not working at the Elekton gatehouse, we hope you can answer some questions—to help solve a mystery."

Frank explained that he and Joe often worked on mysteries and assisted their detective father.

Ken's face brightened. "I'll do my best, fellows," he assured them eagerly.

"Last week," Joe began, "a shabby, green panel truck went to Pritos' Supply Yard and picked up old bricks and lumber. Our friend Tony Prito said there was a boy in the truck who helped the yardman with the loading. Were you the boy?"

"Yes," Ken replied readily.

"Who was the driver?" Frank asked him.

"Mr Docker, the maintenance man at the mill. He said he'd hurt his arm and asked me to help load the stuff." Ken looked puzzled. "Is that part of the mystery?"

"We think it could be," Frank said. "Now, Ken—we've learned since then that one of the bills you gave the yardman is a counterfeit twenty."

Ken's eyes opened wide in astonishment. "A—a counterfeit!" he echoed. "Honest, I didn't know it was, Frank and Joe!"

"Oh, we're sure you didn't," Joe assured him. "Have you any idea who gave Docker the cash?"

Ken told the Hardys he did not know. Then Frank asked:

"What were the old bricks and lumber used for, Ken?"

"Mr Docker told me they were for repair work around the plant. After we got back to the mill, Mr Markel and I stored the load in the basement."

"Is it still there?" asked Frank.

"I guess so," Ken answered. "Up to the time I left, it hadn't been taken out."

The Hardys determined to question Markel and Docker at the first opportunity. Then Frank changed the subject and asked about the day of the picnic when Joe thought he had seen Ken at the window.

"I remember," the younger boy said. "I *did* see you all outside. I never knew you were looking for me."

"When we told Mr Docker," Frank went on, "he said Joe must have been mistaken."

Ken remarked slowly, "He probably was worrying about the plant's security policy. He and Mr Markel were always reminding me not to talk to anybody."

"During the time you were working at the Elekton gatehouse, did you see any strange or suspicious person near either the plant or the mill grounds?" Frank asked.

"No," said Ken in surprise. Curiosity overcoming him, he burst out, "You mean there's some crook loose around here?"

Frank and Joe nodded vigorously. "We're afraid so," Frank told him. "But who, or what he's up to, is what we're trying to find out. When we do, we'll explain everything."

Joe then asked Ken if he had seen anyone in the area of the mill with a bow and arrow.

"A bow and arrow?" Ken repeated. "No, I never did. I sure would've remembered that!"

Frank nodded and switched to another line of questioning. "When you delivered envelopes, Ken, did you always take them to Mr Victor Peters?"

"Yes," Ken answered.

The Hardys learned further that Ken's delivery trips always had been to Bayport—sometimes to the Parker Building, and sometimes to other office buildings in the business section.

"Did Mr Peters meet you in the lobby every time?" Frank queried.

"That's right."

"What was in the envelopes?" was Joe's next question.

"Mr Markel said they were bulletins and forms to be printed for Elekton."

"Were the envelopes always marked confidential?" Joe asked.

"Yes."

"Probably everything is that Elekton sends out," Frank said.

"Sounds like a complicated delivery arrangement to me," Joe declared.

Ken admitted that he had not thought much about it at the time, except that he had assumed Mr Peters relayed the material to the printing company.

Frank and Joe glanced at each other. Both remembered Frank's surmise that the bulky Manila envelopes had not contained bona fide Elekton papers at all!

"What does Mr Peters look like?" asked Joe, a note of intense excitement in his voice.

"Average height and stocky, with a sharp nose. Sometimes he'd be wearing sunglasses."

"Stocky and a sharp nose," Frank repeated. "Sunglasses." Meaningfully he asked Joe, "Whom does that description fit?"

Joe jumped to his feet. "The man who gave Chet the counterfeit twenty at the railroad station!"

The Hardys had no doubt now that the mysterious Victor Peters must be a passer for the counterfeit ring!

· 16 ·

A Night Assignment

GREATLY excited at this valuable clue to the counterfeiters, Frank asked, "Ken, who gave Mr Markel the
envelopes for Victor Peters?"

"I'm sorry, fellows, I don't know."

The Hardys speculated on where Peters was living.
Was it somewhere near Bayport?

Joe's eyes narrowed. "Ken," he said, "this morning
we found out that sometimes you'd ride up that dirt
road to the deserted farmhouse. Was it for any particular reason?"

"Yes," Ken replied. "Mr Markel told me a poor old
man was staying in the house, and a couple of times a
week I was sent there to leave a box of food on the front
porch."

"Did you ever see the 'poor old man'?" Frank asked.
"Or the green panel truck?"

The Hardys were not surprised when the answer to
both questions was No. They suspected the "poor old
man" was Peters hiding out there and that he had made
sure the truck was out of sight whenever Ken was
expected.

The brothers were silent, each puzzling over the
significance of what they had just learned. If the truck

was used by the counterfeiters, how did this tie in with its being used for the sabotage operation at Elekton?

"Was The Arrow in league with the saboteurs? Did he also have something to do with the envelopes sent to Victor Peters?" Joe asked himself.

Frank wondered, "Is The Arrow—or a confederate of his working at Elekton—the person responsible for the warnings, the attack on us, and the tampering with the *Sleuth*?"

"Ken," Frank said aloud, "I think you'd better come and stay with us for a while, until we break this case. Maybe you can help us."

He did not want to mention it to Ken, but the possibility had occurred to him that the boy might be in considerable danger if the counterfeiters suspected that he had given the Hardys any information about Victor Peters.

Ken was delighted with the idea, and Mrs Smith, who knew of Fenton Hardy and his sons, gave permission for her young charge to go.

As a precaution, Frank requested the kindly woman to tell any stranger asking for Ken Blake that he was "visiting friends."

"I'll do that," she agreed.

Ken rode on the back seat of Joe's motorcycle on the trip to High Street. He was warmly welcomed by Mrs Hardy and Aunt Gertrude.

"I hope you enjoy your stay here," said Mrs Hardy, who knew that Frank and Joe had a good reason for inviting Ken. But neither woman asked questions in his presence.

"Your father probably will be out all day," Mrs Hardy told her sons. "He'll phone later."

While lunch was being prepared, Frank called police headquarters to give Chief Collig a report on what had happened at the deserted farmhouse.

"I'll notify the FBI," the chief said. "I'm sure they'll want to send men out there to examine that truck and take fingerprints. Elekton," the chief added, "had no record of any employee answering The Arrow's description."

"We're working on a couple of theories," Frank confided. "But nothing definite so far."

After lunch the Hardys decided their next move was to try to find out more about the contents of the envelopes Ken had delivered to Peters.

"We could ask Elekton officials straight out," Joe suggested.

His brother did not agree. "Without tangible evidence to back us up, we'd have to give too many reasons for wanting to know."

Finally Frank hit on an idea. He telephoned Elekton, asked for the accounting department, and inquired where the company had its printing done. The accounting clerk apparently thought he was a salesman, and gave him the information.

Frank hung up. "What did they say?" Joe asked impatiently.

"All Elekton's printing is done on the premises!"

"That proves it!" Joe burst out. "The set-up with Ken delivering envelopes to Peters isn't a legitimate one and has nothing to do with Elekton business."

Meanwhile Ken, greatly mystified, had been listening

intently. Now he spoke up. "Jeepers, Frank and Joe, have I been doing something wrong?" he asked worriedly.

In their excitement the Hardys had almost forgotten their guest. Frank turned to him apologetically. "Not you, Ken. We're trying to figure out who has."

Just then the Hardys heard the familiar chug of the Queen pulling up outside. The brothers went out to the porch with Ken. Chet leaped from his jalopy and bounded up to them. His chubby face was split with a wide grin.

"Get a load of this!" He showed them a badge with his picture on it. "I'll have to wear it every day when I start work. Everybody has to wear one before he can get into the plant," he added. "Even the president of Elekton!"

Suddenly Chet became aware of Ken Blake. "Hello!" the plump boy greeted him in surprise. Ken smiled, and the Hardys told their friend of the morning's adventure.

"Boy!" Chet exclaimed. "Things are starting to pop! So you found that green truck!"

Suddenly Joe noticed a strange look cross his brother's face.

"Chet," Frank said excitedly, "did you say *everybody* must show identification to enter Elekton's grounds?"

"Yes—everybody," Chet answered positively.

"What are you getting at, Frank?" his brother asked quickly.

"Before yesterday's explosion, when we saw the gate guard admit the green truck, the driver didn't stop—didn't show any identification at all!"

"That's true!" Joe exclaimed. "Mr Markel doesn't seem to be the careless type, though."

"I know," Frank went on. "If the green truck was sneaking in explosives—what better way than to let the driver zip right through."

Joe stared at his brother. "You mean Markel deliberately let the truck go by? That he's in league with the saboteurs, or the counterfeiters, or both?"

As the others listened in astonishment, Frank replied, "I have more than a hunch he is—and Docker too. It would explain a lot."

Joe nodded in growing comprehension. "It sure would!"

"How?" demanded Chet.

Joe took up the line of deduction. "Markel himself told Ken the envelopes were for the printer. Why did Docker say Ken wasn't at the mill the day I saw him? And what was the real reason for his being discharged?"

"I'm getting it," Chet interjected excitedly. "Those men were trying to keep you from questioning Ken. Why?"

"Perhaps because of what Ken could tell us, if we happened to ask him about the envelopes he delivered," Joe replied. Then he asked Ken if Markel and Docker knew that Joe had picked up the envelope on the day of the near accident.

"I didn't say anything about that," Ken replied. The boy's face wore a perplexed, worried look. "You mean Mr Docker and Mr Markel might be—crooks! They didn't act that way."

"I agree," Frank said. "And we still have no proof.

We'll have to see if we can find some—one way or another."

The Hardys reflected on the other mysterious happenings. "The green truck," Frank said, "could belong to the gatehouse men, since it seems to be used for whatever their scheme is, and *they* are hiding it at the deserted farmhouse."

"Also," Joe put in, "if Victor Peters is the 'old man,' he's probably an accomplice."

"And," Frank continued, "don't forget that the bike Ken used was available to both Docker and Markel to deliver the warning note. The arrow shooting occurred near the mill; the attack on us in the woods that night was near the mill. The warning note found in Chet's car was put there after Markel told him to go to the front gate. The guard probably lied to Chet the first day we went to the mill—he never did phone the personnel department."

"Another thing," Joe pointed out. "Both men are more free to come and go than someone working in the plant."

There was silence while the Hardys concentrated on what their next move should be.

"No doubt about it," Frank said finally. "Everything seems to point towards the mill as the place to find the answers."

"And the only way to be sure," Joe added, "is to go and have a look around it ourselves. How about tonight?"

Frank and Chet agreed, and the boys decided to wait until it was fairly dark. "I'll call Tony and see if he can go with us," Frank said. "We'll need his help."

Tony was eager to accompany the trio. "Sounds as if you're hitting the root of the mystery," he remarked, when Frank had brought him up to date.

"We hope so."

Later, Joe outlined a plan whereby they might ascertain if Peters *was* an accomplice of Docker and Markel, and at the same time make it possible for them to get into the mill.

"Swell idea," Frank said approvingly. "Better brush up on your voice-disguising technique!"

Joe grinned. "I'll practise."

Just before supper Mr Hardy phoned to say that he would not be returning home until later that night.

"Making progress, Dad?" asked Frank, who had taken the call.

"Could be, son," the detective replied. "That's why I'll be delayed. Tell your mother and Gertrude not to worry."

"Okay. And, Dad—Joe and I will be doing some sleuthing tonight with Chet and Tony to try out a few new ideas *we* have."

"Fine. But watch your step!"

About eight-thirty that evening Chet and Tony pulled up to the Hardy home in the Queen.

Ken Blake went with the brothers to the door. "See you later, Ken," Frank said, and Joe added, "I know you'd like to come along, but we don't want you taking any unnecessary risks."

The younger boy looked wistful. "I wish I could do something to help you fellows."

"There *is* a way you can help," Frank told him.

At that moment Mrs Hardy and Aunt Gertrude came into the hall. Quickly Frank drew Ken aside and whispered something to him.

Secret Signal

WITH rising excitement, Frank, Joe, Chet and Tony drove off through the dusk towards the old mill.

Chet came to a stop about one hundred yards from the beginning of the road leading to the gatehouse. He and Tony jumped out. They waved to the Hardys, then disappeared into the woods.

Joe took the wheel of the jalopy. "Now, part two of our plan. I hope it works."

The brothers quickly rode to the service station where they had been that morning. Joe parked and hurried to the outdoor telephone booth nearby. From his pocket he took a slip of paper on which Ken had jotted down the night telephone number of the Elekton gatehouse.

Joe dialled the number, then covered the mouthpiece with his handkerchief to muffle his voice.

A familiar voice answered, "Gatehouse. Markel speaking."

Joe said tersely, "Peters speaking. Something has gone wrong. Both of you meet me outside the Parker Building. Make it snappy!" Then he hung up.

When Joe returned to the Queen, Frank had turned it round and they were ready to go. They sped back towards the mill and in about ten minutes had the jalopy parked out of sight in the shadows of the trees where the dirt road joined the paved one.

The brothers, keeping out of sight among the trees, ran to join Chet and Tony who were waiting behind a large oak near the edge of the gatehouse grounds.

"It worked!" Tony reported excitedly. "About fifteen minutes ago the lights in the mill went out, and Markel and Docker left in a hurry."

"On foot?" Joe asked.

"Yes."

"Good. If they have to take a bus or cab to town, it'll give us more time," Frank said.

Tony and Chet were given instructions about keeping watch outside while the Hardys inspected the mill. The brothers explained where the Queen was parked, in case trouble should arise and their friends had to go for help.

Frank and Joe approached the mill cautiously. It was dark now, but they did not use flashlights. Though confident that the gatehouse was deserted, they did not wish to take any chances. As they neared the building the Hardys could see that the shutters were tightly closed. Over the sound of the wind in the trees came the rumble of the turning mill wheel.

The Hardys headed for the door. They had just mounted the steps when the rumbling sound of the wheel ceased.

In the silence both boys looked around, perplexed. "I thought it had been fixed," Joe whispered. "Seemed okay the other day."

"Yes. But last time we were here at night the wheel

stopped when we were about this distance away from it," Frank observed.

Thoughtfully the boys stepped back from the mill entrance to a point where they could see the wheel. They stood peering at it through the darkness. Suddenly, with a dull rumble, it started to turn again!

Mystified, the Hardys advanced towards the gatehouse and stopped at the entrance. In a short while the wheel stopped.

"Hm!" Joe murmured. "Just like one of those electric-eye doors."

"Exactly!" Frank exclaimed, snapping his fingers. "I'll bet the wheel's *not* broken—it's been rigged up as a warning signal to be used at night! When someone approaches the mill, the path of the invisible beam is broken and the wheel stops. The lack of noise is enough for anyone inside to notice, and also, the lights would go out because the generator is powered by the wheel."

The Hardys went on a quick search for the origin of the light beam. Frank was first to discover that it was camouflaged in the flour-barrel ivy planter. Beneath a thin covering of earth, and barely concealed, were the heavy batteries, wired in parallel, which produced the current necessary to operate the light source for the electric eye.

The stopping and starting of the wheel was further explained when Frank found, screened by a bushy shrub, a small post with a tiny glass mirror fastened on its side.

"That's the complete secret of the signal!" he exclaimed. "This is one of the mirrors a photo-electric cell system would use. With several of these hidden mirrors, they've made a light-ring around the mill so that an intruder from any side would break the beam. The barrel that contains the battery power also contains the eye that completes the circuit."

"I'll bet Markel and Docker rigged this up," Joe said excitedly. "Which means there must be something in the mill they want very badly to keep secret! We must find a way inside!"

The Hardys did not pull the wires off the battery connection, since they might have need of the warning system. Quietly and quickly the brothers made a circuit of the mill, trying doors and first-floor windows, in hopes of finding one unlocked. But none was.

"We can't break in," Joe muttered.

Both boys were aware that time was precious—the men might return shortly. The young sleuths made another circle of the mill. This time they paused to stare at the huge wheel, which was turning once more.

"Look!" Joe whispered tensely, pointing to an open window-shaped space above the wheel.

"It's our only chance to get inside," Frank stated. "We'll try climbing up."

The Hardys realized it would not be easy to reach the opening. Had there been a walkway on top of the wheel, as there was in many mills, climbing it would have been relatively simple.

The brothers came to a quick decision: to manœuvre one of the paddles on the wheel until it was directly below the ledge of the open space, then stop the motion. During the short interval which took place between the stop and start of the wheel, they hoped to climb by way of the paddles to the top and gain entrance to the mill.

Joe ran back through the beam, breaking it, while Frank clambered over a pile of rocks across the water to the wheel. It rumbled to a stop, one paddle aligned with the open space above. By the time Joe returned, Frank had started to climb up, pulling himself from paddle to paddle by means of the metal side struts. Joe followed close behind.

The boys knew they were taking a chance in climbing up the wet, slippery, mossy wheel. They were sure there must be a timing-delay switch somewhere in the electric-eye circuit. Could they beat it, or would they be tossed off into the dark rushing water?

"I believe I can get to the top paddle and reach the opening before the timer starts the wheel turning again. But can Joe?" Frank thought. "Hurry!" he cried out to his brother.

Doggedly the two continued upwards. Suddenly Joe's hand slipped on a slimy patch of moss. He almost lost his grip, but managed to cling desperately to the edge of the paddle above his head, both feet dangling in mid-air.

"Frank!" he hissed through clenched teeth.

His brother threw his weight to the right. Holding tight with his left hand to a strut, he reached down and grasped Joe's wrist. Joe locked his fingers on Frank's wrist, and let go with his other hand.

Frank swung him out away from the wheel. As Joe swung himself back, he managed to regain his footing and get a firm hold on the paddle supports.

"Whew!" said Joe. "Thanks!"

The boys resumed the climb, spurred by the thought

that the sluice gate would re-open any second and start the wheel revolving.

Frank finally reached the top paddle. Stretching his arms upwards, he barely reached the sill of the opening. The old wood was rough and splintering, but felt strong enough to hold his weight.

"Here goes!" he thought, and sprang away from the paddle.

At the same moment, with a creaking rumble, the wheel started to move!

·18·

The Hidden Room

WHILE Frank clung grimly to the sill, Joe, below him, knew he must act fast to avoid missing the chance to get off, and perhaps be crushed beneath the turning wheel. He leaped upwards with all his might.

Joe's fingers barely grasped the ledge, but he managed to hang on to the rough surface beside his brother. Then together they pulled themselves up and over the sill through the open space.

In another moment they were standing inside the second floor of the building. Rickety boards creaked under their weight. Still not wishing to risk the use of their flashlights, the Hardys peered around in the darkness.

"I think we're in the original grinding room," Frank whispered, as he discerned the outlines of two huge stone cylinders in the middle of the room.

"You're right," said Joe. "There's the old grain hopper." He pointed to a chute leading down to the grinding stones.

Though many years had passed since the mill had been used to produce flour, the harsh, dry odour of grain still lingered in the air. In two of the corners were cots and a set of crude shelves for clothes. Suddenly the boys' hearts jumped. A loud clattering noise came from directly below. Then, through a wide crack in the floor, shone a yellow shaft of light!

"Someone else must be here!" Joe said in a low voice.

The Hardys stood motionless, hardly daring to breathe, waiting for another sound. Who *was* in the suddenly lighted room?

The suspense was unbearable. Finally the brothers tiptoed over and peered through the wide crack. Straightening up, Frank observed, "Can't see anyone. We'd better go and investigate."

Fearful of stumbling in the inky darkness, the boys now turned on their flashlights but shielded them with their hands. Cautiously they found their way to a door. It opened into a short passageway which led down a narrow flight of steps.

Soon Frank and Joe were in another small hall. Ahead was a partially opened door, with light streaming from it.

Every nerve taut, the young sleuths advanced. Frank edged up to the door and looked in.

"Well? What is it?" Joe hissed. To his utter astonishment, Frank gave a low chuckle, and motioned him forward.

"For Pete's sake!" Joe grinned.

Inside, perched on a chipped grindstone, was a huge white cat. Its tail twitched indignantly. An overturned lamp lay on a table.

The Hardys laughed in relief. "Our noise-maker and lamplighter!" Frank said, as the boys entered the room.

"The cat must have knocked over the lamp and clicked the switch."

Although the room contained the gear mechanism and the shaft connected to the mill wheel, it was being used as a living area by the present tenants. There were two overstuffed chairs, a table, and a chest of drawers. On the floor, as if dropped in haste, lay a scattered newspaper.

"Let's search the rest of the mill before Markel and Docker get back," Joe suggested. "Nothing suspicious here."

The Hardys started with the top storey of the old building. There they found what was once the grain storage room. Now it was filled with odds and ends of discarded furniture.

"I'm sure nothing's been hidden up here," Frank said.

The other floors yielded no clues as to what Docker and Markel's secret might be.

Frank was beginning to feel rather discouraged. "Maybe our big hunch is all wrong," he muttered unhappily.

Joe refused to give up. "Let's investigate the cellar. Come on!"

The brothers went into the kitchen towards the basement stairway. Suddenly Joe gave a stifled yell. Something had brushed across his trouser legs. Frank swung his light around. The beam caught two round golden eyes staring up at them.

"The white cat!" Joe said sheepishly.

Chuckling, the Hardys continued down into the

damp, cool cellar. It was long and narrow, with only two small windows.

Three walls were of natural stone and mortar. The fourth wall was lined with wooden shelves. Hopefully, Frank and Joe played their flashlights into every corner.

"Hm." There was a note of disappointment in Joe's voice. "Wheelbarrow, shovels, picks—just ordinary equipment."

Frank nodded thoughtfully. "That seems to be all, but where are the old bricks and lumber that Ken said were stored here?"

"I'm sure the stuff was never intended for Elekton," Joe declared. "More likely the mill. But where? On a floor? We haven't seen any signs."

Thoughtfully the boys walked over to inspect the shelves, which held a varied assortment of implements and tools. Frank reached out to pick up a hammer.

To his amazement, he could not lift it. A further quick examination revealed that all the tools were glued to the shelves.

"Joe!" he exclaimed. "There's a special reason for this—and I think it's camouflage!"

"You mean these shelves are movable, and the tools are fastened so that they won't fall off?"

"Yes. Also, I have a feeling this whole section is made of the old lumber from Prito's yard."

"And the bricks?" Joe asked, puzzled.

His brother's answer was terse. "Remember, this mill was used by settlers. In those days many places like this had hidden rooms in case they were attacked by Indians—"

"I get you!" Joe broke in. "Those bricks are in a secret room! The best place to build one in this mill would have been the cellar."

"Right," agreed Frank. "And the only thing unusual here is this shelf set-up. I'll bet it's actually the entrance to the secret room."

"All we have to do is find the opening mechanism," Joe declared.

Using their flashlights, the boys went over every inch of the shelves. These were nailed to a backing of boards. The Hardys pulled and pushed, but nothing happened. Finally, on the bottom shelf near the wall, Frank discovered a knot in the wood. In desperation, he pressed his thumb hard against the knot.

There was the hum of a motor and, as smoothly as though it were moving on greased rails, the middle section of shelves swung inward.

"The door to the secret room!" Frank exclaimed excitedly.

Quickly the boys slipped inside the room and shone their flashlights around. The first thing they noticed was the flooring—recently laid bricks. Frank snapped on a light switch beside the entrance.

The boys blinked in the sudden glare of two high-watt bulbs suspended from the low ceiling. The next instant both of them spotted a small hand-printing press.

"The counterfeiters' workshop!" they cried out.

On a wooden table at the rear of the room were a camera, etching tools, zinc plates, and a large pan with little compartments containing various colours of ink. At the edge of the table was a portable typewriter.

Frank picked up a piece of paper, rolled it into the machine, and typed a few lines. Pulling it out, he showed the paper to Joe.

"This is the same machine as was used to type the warning note Dad got!" Joe exclaimed excitedly. "The counterfeiters must have thought he was on their trail."

"And look over here!" exclaimed Frank, his voice tense. A small pile of twenty-dollar bills lay among the equipment. "They're fakes," he added, scrutinizing the bills. "They're the same as Chet's and Tony's."

Joe made another startling discovery. In one corner stood a bow, with the string loosened and carefully wound around the handgrip. A quiver of three hunting arrows leaned against the wall nearby.

Excitedly Joe pulled one out. "The same type that was fired at the girls," he observed. "This must belong to The Arrow!"

"Docker matches his description," Frank pointed out enthusiastically. "He could easily have coloured his hair grey."

The Hardys were thrilled at the irrefutable evidence all around them. "Now we know why Markel and Docker rigged the mill wheel—to give a warning signal when they're working in this room!"

"Also, we now have a good idea what was being sent to Peters in the envelopes—phoney twenty-dollar bills!"

"Let's get Dad and Chief Collig here!" Joe urged,

stuffing several of the counterfeits into one of his pockets.

As the boys turned to leave, the lights in the secret room went out. Frank and Joe froze. They realized the mill wheel had stopped turning.

"The signal!" Joe said grimly. "Someone is coming!"

· 19 ·

Underground Chase

THE Hardys knew this was the signal for them to get out of the secret room—and fast! As they hurried into the cellar, the lights came on again. With hearts beating faster, they started for the stairway. But before the boys reached it, they heard the mill door being unlocked, then heavy footsteps pounded overhead.

"Docker!" a man's voice called. "Markel! Where are you!"

The Hardys listened tensely, hoping for a chance to escape unseen. When they heard the man cross the ground floor and go upstairs, Joe whispered, "Let's make a break for it!"

The boys dashed to the steps. They could see a crack of light beneath the closed door to the kitchen. Suddenly the light vanished, and the rumble of the mill wheel ceased.

The Hardys stopped in their tracks. "Somebody else is coming!" Frank muttered. "Probably Docker and Markel. We're trapped!"

Again the brothers heard the mill door open. Two men were talking loudly and angrily. Then came the sound of footsteps clattering down the stairs to the first fl

"Peters!" The boys recognized Docker's voice. "Where in blazes were you? We waited for you as long as we could."

Frank and Joe nudged each other. Victor Peters *was* in league with the gatehouse men!

"What do you mean? I told you I'd meet you here at eleven," snarled Peters.

"You must be nuts!" retorted Markel. "You called here an hour ago and said there was trouble and to meet *you* at the Parker Building."

Peters's tone grew menacing. "Something's fishy. I didn't phone. You know I'd use the two-way radio. What's the matter with you guys, anyway?"

"Listen!" Markel snapped. "*Somebody* called here and said he was you. The voice did sound sort of fuzzy, but I didn't have a chance to ask questions—he hung up on me. I thought that maybe your radio had conked out."

The Hardys, crouched on the cellar stairs, could feel the increasing tension in the room above. Docker growled, "Something funny *is* going on. Whoever phoned must be on to us, or suspect enough to want to get in here and snoop around."

"The Feds! We'll have to scram!" said Markel, with more than a trace of fear in his voice. "Come on! Let's get moving!"

"Not so fast, Markel!" Docker barked. "We're not ditching the stuff we've made. We'll have a look around first—starting with the cellar."

The men strode into the kitchen. Below, Frank grabbed Joe. "We've no choice now. Into the secret room!"

Quickly the brothers ran back into the workshop. Frank pulled the door behind him and slid the heavy bolt into place.

Tensely the brothers pressed against the door as the three men came downstairs into the basement. Frank and Joe could hear them moving around, searching for signs of an intruder.

"I'd better check the rest of the mill," Docker said brusquely. "You two get the plates and the greenbacks. Go out through the tunnel, and I'll meet you at the other end. We'll wait there for Blum to pay us off, then vamoose."

"We're in a fix, all right," Joe said under his breath. "What tunnel are they talking about?"

"And who's Blum?" Frank wondered.

The boys heard the hum of the motor that opened the secret door. But the bolt held it shut.

"The mechanism won't work!" Markel rasped.

"Maybe it's just stuck," said Peters.

The men began pounding on the wood.

"What's going on?" Docker demanded as he returned.

"We can't budge this tricky door you dreamed up," Peters complained.

"There's nothing wrong with the door, you block-heads!" Docker shouted. "Somebody's in the room! Break down the door!"

In half a minute his order was followed by several sharp blows.

"Oh, that's great!" Joe groaned. "They're using axes!"

"We won't have long to figure a way out," Frank said wryly.

"Way out!" Joe scoffed. "There isn't any!"

Frank's mind raced. "Hey! They said something about leaving through a tunnel! It must lead out from here."

Frantically the Hardys searched for another exit from the secret room. They crawled on the floor, and pried up one brick after another looking for a ring that might open a trap door.

"Nothing!" Joe said desperately.

All the while the men in the cellar kept battering away at the door. "Good thing that old lumber is such hard wood," Frank thought. "But they'll break through any minute."

"Look!" Joe pointed. "Over there. Under the bench!"

Frank noticed a shovel lying beneath the worktable. The boys pushed it aside and saw that the wall behind the table was partially covered with loose dirt. On a hunch, Frank grabbed the shovel and started to dig into the dirt.

"This dirt might have been put here to hide the entrance to the tunnel!" he gasped.

"It better be!" His brother clawed frantically at the dirt.

At the same moment there was a loud splintering noise. The Hardys looked round. A large crack had appeared in the bolted door.

One of the men outside yelled, "A couple more blows and we'll be in."

Frank dug furiously. Suddenly his shovel opened u

a small hole in the crumbly dirt. Joe scooped away with his hands. Finally there was a space big enough for the boys to squeeze through. Without hesitation, Frank wriggled in, then Joe.

From behind them came a tremendous crash and the sound of ripping wood. Markel's voice shouted, "Into the tunnel! After 'em!"

The Hardys heard no more as they pushed ahead on hands and knees into the damp darkness of an earthen passageway.

Joe was about to call out to his brother when he became aware that someone was crawling behind him. "No room here for a knockdown fight," he thought, wondering if the pursuer were armed.

The young detective scrambled on as fast as he could in the narrow, twisting tunnel. He managed to catch up to Frank, and with a push warned him to go at top speed.

"Somebody's after us!" Joe hissed. "If only we can outdistance him!"

The underground route was a tortuous, harrowing one. The Hardys frequently scraped knees and shoulders against sharp stones in the tunnel floor and walls. They had held on to their flashlights, but did not dare turn them on.

"This passageway is endless!" Frank thought. The close, clammy atmosphere made it increasingly difficult for his brother and he to breathe.

Joe thought uneasily, "What if we hit a blind alley and are stuck in here?"

The boys longed to stop and catch their breath, but they could hear the sounds of pursuit growing nearer, and forced themselves onward faster than ever.

Frank wondered if Chet and Tony had seen the men enter the mill and had gone for help.

"We'll need it," he thought grimly.

Suddenly the brothers came to another turn and the ground began to slope sharply upwards.

"Maybe we're getting close to the end," Frank conjectured hopefully.

Spurred by possible freedom, he put on a burst of speed. Joe did the same. A moment later Frank stopped unexpectedly and Joe bumped into him.

"What's the matter? Why have you stopped?" he barely whispered.

"Dead end," reported his brother.

Squeezing up beside Frank, Joe reached out and touched a pile of stones blocking their path. The boys were now able to hear the heavy breathing of their pursuer.

"Let's move these stones," Frank urged.

Both Hardys worked with desperate haste to pull the barrier down. They heaved thankful sighs when a draught of fresh air struck their faces.

"The exit!" Joe whispered in relief.

The brothers wriggled quickly through the opening they had made and found themselves in a rock-walled space.

"It's the cave by the river, Joe!" Frank cried out. "Someone put back the rocks we removed!"

The boys clicked on their flashlights and started towards the entrance of the cave.

"We beat 'em to it!" Joe exclaimed.

"That's what you think!" came a harsh voice from the entrance.

The glare from two flashlights almost blinded the Hardys. Docker and Markel, with drawn revolvers, had stepped into the cave.

Solid Evidence

For a second the two armed men stared in disbelief at Frank and Joe. "The Hardy boys!" Docker snarled. "So you're the snoopers we've trapped!"

There was a scuffling in the tunnel behind the boys. A stocky man, huffing and puffing, emerged from the tunnel. The Hardys recognized him instantly: the counterfeit passer, Victor Peters.

The newcomer gaped at the Hardys. "What are *they* doing here?"

"A good question!" Markel snapped at his accomplice. "You told us on the two-way radio you'd locked 'em up with the truck."

Peters whined, "I *did*. They must've broken out."

"Obviously." Docker gave him a withering look.

Frank and Joe realized that Peters had not returned to the old farmhouse.

Docker whirled on them. "How *did* you escape?"

The boys looked at him coldly. "That's for you to find out," Joe retorted.

"It's a good thing Markel and I decided to head 'em off at the cave," Docker added angrily. "Otherwise they would have escaped again."

The Hardys could see that the men were nervous and edgy. "I'm not the only one who made a mistake," Peters growled. "I told you a couple of days ago to get rid of that kid Ken when these pests started asking about him, and then found the tunnel. We could have thrown 'em off the scent!"

While the men argued, the Hardys kept on the alert for a chance to break away. Markel's eye caught the movement, and he levelled his revolver. "Don't be smart!" he ordered. "You're covered."

Peters continued his tirade against his confederates. "Docker, you should've finished these Hardys off when you put 'em in the boat that night! And you"—Peters turned on Markel—"*you* could have planted a dynamite charge in their boat instead of just monkeying with the throttle."

The Hardys, meanwhile, were thankful for the precious minutes gained by the men's dissension. "Tony and Chet might come back in time with help," Joe thought.

Simultaneously, Frank hoped that Ken Blake had carried out his whispered instructions.

Docker glanced nervously at his watch. "Blum ought to be here," he fumed.

"Who's Blum?" Frank asked suddenly. "One of your counterfeiting pals?"

Docker, Markel and Peters laughed scornfully. "No," said Markel. "We're the only ones in our exclusive society. Paul Blum doesn't know anything about our—er—mill operation, but it was through him we got the jobs at the gatehouse. The whole deal really paid off double."

Docker interrupted him with a warning. "Don't blab so much!"

Markel sneered. "Why not? What I say won't do these smart alecks any good."

Joe looked at the guard calmly. "Who paid you to let the green panel truck into Elekton?"

All three men started visibly. "How'd you know that?" Markel demanded.

"Just had a hunch," Joe replied.

The former guard regained his composure. "We'll get our money for that little job tonight."

Frank and Joe felt elated. Paul Blum, whom these men expected, must be the sabotage ring-leader! "So that's what Markel meant by the deal paying off double," Frank thought. "He and Docker working the counterfeit racket on their own—and being in league with the saboteurs."

Frank addressed Markel in an icy tone. "You call blowing up a building a 'little job'?"

The counterfeiters' reactions astonished the Hardys. "*What!*" bellowed Peters, as Docker and Markel went ashen.

Joe snorted. "You expect us to believe you didn't *know* explosives were in that truck?"

Victor Peters was beside himself with rage. "*Fools!*" he shrilled at Docker and Markel. "You let yourselves be used by saboteurs? This whole state will be crawling with police and federal agents."

The gatehouse men, though shaken, kept their revolvers trained on the Hardys. "Never mind," Docker muttered. "Soon as Blum shows up we'll get out of here and lie low for a while."

Frank and Joe learned also that Docker and Markel actually were brothers, but the two refused to give their real names.

"You, Docker, are known as The Arrow, aren't you?" Frank accused him.

"Yeah. Next time I'll use *you* boys for targets!" the man retorted threateningly.

The Hardys kept egging the men on to further admissions. Docker and Markel had been approached several months before by Blum who tipped them off to good-paying jobs at the Elekton gatehouse. Docker had cleverly forged references and identification for Markel and himself.

As soon as he and Markel had obtained the jobs, Blum had instructed them to buy the truck second-hand in another state, and told them only that Markel was to lend Blum the truck on a certain day when notified, let him through the gate, then out again soon after closing time. The guard would be handsomely paid to do this.

When Markel and Docker had become settled in the mill, the two had discovered the secret room and tunnel, which once had a been settlers' escape route. The men had wasted no time in setting it up for their counterfeiting racket, and often used the nondescript green truck to sneak in the required equipment.

"Who rigged up the electric-eye signal?" Frank queried.

"My work," Docker replied proudly.

As the boys had surmised, Peters, an old acquaintance of theirs, was "the old man" at the deserted farmhouse. When the boys had left the mill that morning